ERWIN MORTIER (born 1965) made his mark in 1999 with his debut novel *Marcel*, which was awarded several prizes in Belgium and the Netherlands, and received acclaim throughout Europe. In the following years he quickly built up a reputation as one of the leading authors of his generation. His novel *While the Gods Were Sleeping* received the AKO Literature Prize, one of the most prestigious awards in the Netherlands. His latest work, *Stammered Songbook*, a raw yet tender elegy about illness and loss, was met with unanimous praise. Mortier's evocative descriptions bring past worlds brilliantly to life.

ERWIN MORTIER

MY FELLOW SKIN

Translated from the Dutch by
Ina Rilke

PUSHKIN PRESS
LONDON

Pushkin Press
71-75 Shelton Street, London WC2H 9JQ

Original text © 2011 by Erwin Mortier.
In a licence from De Bezige Bij, Amsterdam.

English translation © Ina Rilke, 2003

My Fellow Skin first published in Dutch as *Mijn tweede huid* by
Uitgeverij J. M. Meulenhoff bv, Amsterdam in 2000

This translation first published in 2003 by Harvill Secker
First published by Pushkin Press in 2014

0 0 1

ISBN 978 1 782270 19 5

Set in Monotype Baskerville
by Tetragon, London

Printed and bound by
CPI Group (UK) Ltd., Croydon CRO 4YY

www.pushkinpress.com

MY FELLOW SKIN

PART I

CHAPTER I

I T WAS IN THE DAYS BEFORE I had learned to talk
properly. Hardly anything had a name, everything was
body. Standing in front of the mirror my father drew the
razor blade over his cheeks, stretched his neck and gently
scraped the foam from his Adam's apple. He eyed his face
narrowly from under his lashes, the curve of upper lip, the
lower lip, the chin.

His dressing gown hung loosely over his shoulders. Behind
him, in the bath, I was rocking in the waves he had made
getting out, pulling the water with him. The solemn silence
between him and his reflection gave everything an extraordinary clarity. I can still see, as sharply as I did then, the wet hairs
bunching on his shins. In the mirror, above the slumbering
sex and milk-white stomach, a track of curly hair rose from
his navel to fan out on the shallows of his chest, where I could
see his heart beating.

He had run the bath until it was half-full. He had strewn
soapflakes in the water and had rinsed the sting from my
eyes when he washed my hair. Clean-shaven now, he scooped
water over his cheeks, turned to face me and held out his
hands.

"Come on, arms up now," he said.

I lolled weightless in his arms. I shook in all my joints as he dabbed at my ears with a clean towel and rubbed my skull dry. I clung to his calves.

Sitting, legs splayed, on the lowered lavatory seat, he waited for me to steady myself, took my hands in his and ran the back of his thumb across my nails. "Let's check," he said, "and see if all ten of them are still there." And if there was any dirt left underneath.

Finally he dressed me in my bathrobe and opened the door to let me out.

*

I stepped out of the bathroom like a prince, into the dusky corridor. Ahead of me, past doors behind which rooms drowsed, the corridor tunnelled through the house. Some rooms were familiar, others not. To the left was the door to the cellar, concealing a flight of brick steps, damp and glistening with salt crystals. To the right was the playroom with the building blocks and the dolls I didn't trust because they remained sitting down, even when I wasn't looking.

There were so many things waiting to be baptised. Anything without a word to it was too pagan and savage to be left alone. I had to lay my finger on everything within reach.

I could smell the kitchen, a whiff of drains and of hams in gingham sacks hanging from hooks in the rafters.

Someone called my name. A hand detached itself from the shadows by the chimney piece and lightly brushed my cheek, but I did not stop. From the far side of the stove I heard the pious creak of a wicker chair. Next thing I knew, my ear was given a playful tweak.

My mother busied herself taking plates from the cupboard and theatrically banging them down on the table.

"Anton," she cried. "Anton, little man. Dancing about in your bare feet like that—you'll fetch up with a tummy ache."

I took no notice. It was a time for cutting cords and chasing hens in the yard, even though that wasn't allowed.

In the recesses of the house, where the corridor forked in two and the light was rarely switched on, I felt a stab of fear. This place, inhabited by aunts and cousins in summer but deserted and soulless when they were gone, was home to the dreaded grandfather clock. Its slow beat always seemed to threaten me as I approached, but when I tiptoed past, it continued ticking quite harmlessly. Now the clock was silent. My father had stopped it, so no-one would be disturbed by the quarter-hourly chimes it sent ringing through the rooms.

*

He knew what was best for everyone in the house. He knew who wouldn't mind the morning sunlight and who was more partial to the west-facing rooms with the rambler rose outside the window, scenting the air after every shower as if death were at its heels. Come the lazy nights of August with the occasional thunderstorms, I would hear him get up to rescue cousin Flora from the cellar, where he would find her cowering in the space between the freezer and the bottle racks with an upturned saucepan on her head. He would unclench the rosary from her fingers, lift the saucepan off her hair, put his arms around her and say, "It's not the Germans, Flora. Just a bit of thunder."

11

The things that scared me were not yet inside me, but around me. I sought out my fears to check if they were still there—to make sure they hadn't taken it into their heads to abscond to other places, the better to pounce on me when I least expected. I checked for new shapes in the gloom under the stairs, where the silenced clock filled the air with mute indignation. A door opened a crack and something with worn-down claws padded across the floorboards towards me, wagging its tail. A moist nose snuffling at my toes made me cry out in fearful delight. Not until I cried out again did the hoped-for response come.

"Hear that?" a voice boomed from one of the rooms. "Our little man. Over here, lad. Let's have a look at you."

The soft cooing of amused aunts guided me to the right door.

The three of them were sitting at the round table, drinking gin. There was Michel, who lived with us summer and winter in two separate rooms, enveloped in clouds of snuff and the stale smell of Molly his dog. Next to him sat Odette, a gawky creature with long arms like a praying mantis. At the other side of the table Alice, red-haired and flushed, offered me her unconscionably soft cheek to kiss.

"He's a fine mountaineer already," said Michel, slapping his thighs invitingly. "Watch this."

I planted my feet on top of his, gripped his knees with my hands and walked up his shins.

"Up you go, up you go," the Aunts chanted.

Once at the summit I slid on to his lap. My fingers groped their way up his shirt, button after button, until they reached his chin. Bare skin at last. Stubble. Papery wrinkles. Chapped lips.

He leaned over me to reach for his drink, raised the glass to his lips, took a leisurely gulp and replaced it on the table, out of harm's way.

I put my hands up to his cheeks and smacked them in protest.

"You can't have any of that," the Aunts said, laughing. "Far too strong. You'd mess your trousers."

He pulled faces and gave me broad winks, stuck out his tongue and wagged his head from side to side. "You can't hurt me. You're too little. It's milk you should be drinking. Milk and nothing else."

I can still feel the palm of his hand against the back of my head, his thumb rubbing the hair on my neck the wrong way.

He was about to say something. I saw him swallow and press his lips together, then open his mouth so that his back teeth showed, but there was no sound.

He nodded and nodded, and I nodded along with him. "'Ullo," I cried. "'Ullo, 'ullo, 'ullo."

I could hear his breath rasping against the roof of his mouth, and deeper down, struggling in his larynx to drag the words from his stomach, as though he had to forcibly expel them from his spasming torso.

Suddenly my pleasure capsized and I was gripped by a fathomless fear, no doubt because of the Aunts' shrieks of horror. Everything went dark.

*

Someone, perhaps my father, snatched me from his lap. Someone else, probably my mother, must have called the doctor.

He had fallen sideways to the floor. Hands flew to mop his brow, straighten his legs and slip a cushion under him, to pull off the slippers, then the socks, and to massage the soles of his feet, which already felt cold.

My mother took me to the kitchen and plied me with milk and chocolate, with crayons and pictures, to distract me from the commotion in the corridor, where someone hurried to answer the doorbell.

A moment later my father came to the kitchen. With his hand on the doorknob and half-hidden behind the door, it was as though he didn't want me to see him. He glanced at my mother, shaking his head.

From elsewhere in the house came the sound of low lamentations. Curtains were drawn. Shutters creaked on their hinges. Our house, Callewijns Hof, at the foot of the dyke along the canal to Bruges, inhabited by us for generations, altered and extended and renovated, had preserved all manner of latches and locks from the past, and now proceeded to shut itself off from the outside world with every one of them.

My mother rose, ran my sticky fingers under the pump and dried them.

"Say night night, sleep tight." And she scooped me up on to her arm.

*

In the parlour the Aunts were settled on the sofa like huge black flies, dabbing at their eyes with fluttery lace-edged handkerchiefs as flimsy as the grief choking their muted voices.

My father was hunched in a corner, half-hidden by the heavy blinds, clutching a huge square of checked cloth in

14

his fists. Compared to the trickle of sorrow shown by his sisters and cousins, the grief deep inside my father was a vast reservoir, swelling and swelling until the dam burst and it all poured forth.

My mother carried me around the room, pausing in front of each mourner. Some were strangers, spectral figures holding their caps on their knees and keeping an unaccustomed silence, fumbling with trouser legs or whispering uneasy my-oh-mys. Oh my.

My father smiled bravely when I pressed my lips to his, and thumbed a sign of the cross on my forehead. The Aunts quickly tucked their hankies in their sleeves, took my face in both hands and offered me their cheeks. There was another ring at the door, and my mother said, "Come, time for bed. Upstairs with you."

She chivvied me up the stairs more hurriedly than usual, wormed my arms into the sleeves of my night shirt as if she were dressing a rag doll, and then tucked me up without giving me a chance to say goodnight to my bears.

The whole regiment of bears sat on the shelf fixed to the wall facing my cot, motionless and adoring, their glass eyes staring and glinting in the glow coming up from a street light.

I was given a hasty goodnight kiss. Left and right of me my mother raised the collapsible sides of the cot. I was in a cage. The net curtains swayed to and fro in front of the screened window, and in the dying light a lost butterfly whirred helplessly against the pane.

*

Until now the days had billowed around me beatifically, and I would seize upon what they had to offer as if I were ferreting for hidden goodies in the Aunts' skirts on birthdays. The hours were puppet shows. They would open on demand to reveal the same familiar scenes again and again. Things waited patiently for me to notice them and acknowledge their existence by giving them names.

But now all sorts of things were going on behind my back. The usual sounds of the night unfurling its landscape, like the lowing of cows on heat, the barking of dogs, the fatherly throb of a barge on the canal beyond the garden wall, were drowned out by footsteps on the cobbles in the front yard.

The wrought iron gate in the archway was given a cautious push, which made it squeal even louder than usual. I could hear wheels rumbling over the cobbles and then the soft purr of an engine, at which moment a beam of surprisingly brilliant light swept across my room, covering my walls with a shifting trellis of leaves and branches.

Car doors were wrenched open, then slammed shut. The beam of light went out. Lips smacked against cheeks. More footsteps, this time on the front doorstep with its little pitched roof. I recognised my father's bass voice, and the high, plaintive tones of my mother. I couldn't tell whether she was laughing or crying.

She was sure to be standing in the doorway, rubbing her hands over her arms, even though it was summer and not at all chilly.

The boot of a car was opened and then closed with a dull thud. Meanwhile someone was hopping lightly down the corridor, singing jauntily, "Down in the hole... down in

16

the hole." The singing stopped suddenly when the umbrella stand fell over with a deafening clatter.

A woman's voice, which I did not recognise, called out in suppressed anger, "Shsh, Anton's already asleep."

The stairwell filled with the hollow echo of all the voices at once. My father shut the front door, I could tell by the scrape of wood across the tiled floor. Once the tumult subsided the voices coming up through the floorboards sounded muffled.

I was wide awake. The idea that things could go on being exactly the same as they were in the dark, despite having their distinctive shapes and features blotted out, gave me a strange sense of restlessness.

When I turned over on my side or on my back, making my sheets rustle and the bars of my cot rattle, I could hear the sound hitting the walls and bouncing back to me.

Later, when my father slipped into my bedroom to see if I was all right, it was as though the room and everything in it, including myself, took a deep breath. He was surprised to find me wide awake, crawling out from the covers to greet him.

He lowered the side of the cot, sat down on the edge of the mattress and enfolded me in his arms.

I put my hands on his wrists and looked up. The stubble on the underside of his chin felt prickly through my hair.

It must have been very late, later than ever before. It was the dead of night, and I'd have been unconsciously floating towards morning had not the natural order of things been disturbed, leaving us stranded. He did not tell me a story. He did not wind up the music box on the bedside table and talk to me until the tune started. He did not speak at all, just held me close to his chest.

17

Outside, on the landing, the stairs groaned under the weight of some bulky object being hauled up, tread by tread.

"Over here," I heard my mother say in a low voice, and again I could make out the sound of someone hopping lightly down the corridor. The hopping came to a stop outside my bedroom, and the slit of light under the door was interrupted by a patch of dark, which cast a long shadow across my floor. The same song was being sung, in the same nasal voice as before, but softer now, "Down in the hole, down in the hole." Then it tailed off.

"Night night," my father said, lifting me up on his arm so that I might stroke each of my bears in turn. Furry ears, dry snouts against the palm of my hand, and the cool glass of their staring eyes.

"Night night," I said imperiously, as though everything were still at my command.

My father pulled up the covers and tucked the blanket loosely under the mattress. He gave my fingers a joky nibble when I touched his lips in the dark. I laughed out loud. He shut the door gently behind him.

I gripped the sheet with both fists and drew it up around my chin. I stretched out comfortably. Calm had been restored at last. Even the bears, content now they had received their due, would be smiling down at me from their shelf.

If I lay there long enough without moving a muscle or blinking an eye, they'd think I was asleep and start talking to each other in the dark. They'd be shy at first, but soon they'd be chattering happily.

I slipped my hands under my pillow. The world fell silent. My eyelids grew heavy. The only sound was the wind riffling the leafy crown of the beech tree. The night filled up with all the words I didn't yet know, with all the things that had yet to be touched and realised.

I turned over and shut my eyes.

"Night, night," I repeated, "night, night."

CHAPTER 2

THE TWITTER OF BIRDS roused me from sleep. Bees buzzed around the creeper outside. In the afternoon warmth, shafts of the brightest light jutted in through the window, flooding the floor and making the dust float in the heat. Inside the room the floorboards began to expand around the nails securing them to the beams below. Soon they would emit a persistent ticking or tapping, sometimes so vehemently that the filler burst out of the cracks with a loud pop and the falling fragments danced over the floor.

A small, compact bundle in my nightwear, I kicked impatiently against the bedclothes that granted me little freedom. When I tried spreading my legs, the sheet stretched taut like a sail between my ankles and hips.

"Get up!" I must have cried. Or maybe it was "Pa-pa!"

The echo bouncing back from the walls sounded less hollow than usual, and it was then that I realised, with some alarm, that the door was ajar.

There was the scrape of a foot, a tightening of the covers.

I glimpsed a hand disappearing below the end of my cot. Someone with designs on my bears had ducked away like a flash, and was now lying in wait.

I stared hard at the foot of the bed, as if I would eventually be able to look over the edge and grab the intruder by the scruff of the neck.

We waited. Neither of us dared to move, afraid to make the slightest sound. I could hear his breathing and he could probably hear mine.

From outside came the sounds of early afternoon. I could hear someone tramping about in the yard with clanking pails and the chickens squabbling over the best scraps.

A jolt reminded me of the intruder. Perhaps he'd been crouching there the whole time, perhaps his muscles had gone all rigid and he'd toppled over.

From behind the foot of the bed rose a mop of tousled, chestnut hair, then eyebrows like brushes over dark brown eyes. Holding my gaze, without a hint of shame.

I screwed up my eyes in disbelief. No-one ever came in here except my father, my mother, and on very special occasions one of the Aunts. To pick me up or lie me down or pat me fondly. That was the only kind of stir there was supposed to be.

Everything else was supposed to keep quite still, like my bears on the shelf.

When I opened my eyes again I saw him emerging from his hiding place. His shirt hung out of his trousers. The buckles of his sandals were undone and tinkled around his ankles. He advanced slowly, a sly grin on his face.

"In the hole, down in the hole!" he chanted under his breath.

From the corner of my eye I saw him going down on his knees beside me. The wooden bars rattled loudly as he shook them, and he gave a little laugh of grim amusement.

Then, after a few seconds' tingling silence, came the sound of his voice alarmingly close to my ear. "Anton…" he said, and then, slowly and maliciously, "An-ton-ne-ke," as though he took pride in knowing my pet name and using it against me.

I averted my face crossly and fixed my eyes on the stains of long-evaporated rainwater below the window sill. Sometimes, in the evening twilight, the stains seemed to liquefy and turn into trolls or wizards. If only I could focus on other things for long enough, he would surely go away of his own accord.

Suddenly I felt three fingers trailing across my face, moving from cheek to mouth and up to the eyes. I curled my toes in response to the tickling sensation, blew hard against his hand and twisted my head from side to side.

His fingers closed round my nose like a vice.

My eyes filled with tears, and the pain shot all the way up to the roots of my hair. He dragged me upright. I did not resist. My panting breath moistened his wrist. I struggled with both hands to push him away, but he did not loosen his grip, determined to unscrew my nose from my face.

I didn't want to plead for mercy, I didn't want to cry out, but his fingers dug deeper and deeper into my flesh. I felt sick with pain. My midriff tensed, my lungs filled up almost to bursting, but when my mouth opened wide to scream, a woman's voice, the same one as the night before, seemed to do it for me.

"Roland," she yelled, "Roland, boy... where are you?"

He let go of me at once. My head crashed back on the pillow.

I heard him stomp across the floor and out of the room. The door shuddered on its hinges.

My muscles relaxed, my breathing recovered its familiar rhythm and I rubbed the moisture from my eyes. Elsewhere in the house a tap was turned on, pipes murmured. Somewhere water splashed in a basin.

*

Roland. When my mother took me downstairs he was nowhere to be seen, but there were two unoccupied chairs at the other end of the table, gaping at me menacingly.

It was still dark in the house, and no-one spoke. The Aunts clasped their cups with both hands and drank in silence, pausing briefly between sips to stare blankly into the distance. A thin, strangely cold light entered the room through the crack under the roller blind, making the Aunts' black hairpins stand out from the surrounding gloom.

Everything seemed to be late. The cool of the shuttered rooms downstairs had robbed the hours of their soul. Outside, the back yard would be blazing in the heat of mid-afternoon, while inside a morning atmosphere still reigned. There was the usual bustle to prepare for a new day, even though the day was half-gone already.

Michel was missing. He ought to have been right next to me at the corner of the table with his walking stick propped against his thigh, feeding me my slice of bread, while I sat enthroned in my high chair with my own table-top and potty and the dog looking up at me longingly, whining softly and pawing the air.

My father was nowhere to be seen.

My mother stacked the dishes and carried them to the kitchen. The Aunts leaned back helpfully when she swept up the crumbs from the table with a small brush.

"Eat," she snapped at me in passing. She pushed the bread into my hands.

I nibbled at it listlessly. Everything was eluding me. The table was already being cleared. Only at the far end, well beyond

23

my reach, by the empty chairs, were things left standing: milk and jam and sugar.

*

I heard feet stamping on the stairs, and again the voice of that woman.

"Come here, silly…"

Roland lurched unwillingly into the room at her hand. His hair had been combed flat against his skull and shone as if he'd been given a coat of varnish. The buckles of his sandals were fastened and his shirt was firmly stuffed into his trousers, which had been pulled up almost to his armpits. He resembled a wooden doll, only just come to life, with nothing but strife in mind.

"Sit down at table now. It's always the same with you," his mother snapped while she turned an apologetic smile on the rest of us. She was just as coarsely shaped as her son. She exuded the same sort of menace, like the ominous grey of thunderclouds glowering behind a stand of trees.

I was glad to be sitting in my high chair, for the lofty protection it gave me. He would have to reach up on tiptoe to pinch me, or hoist himself on to the chair next to mine, but to my relief his mother sat down beside me.

"I've left you some cheese," she said absently, "and there's pear treacle, too."

A cushion was stuffed under Roland's bottom and he eyed me triumphantly from the other side of the table as if it were his own property. While his mother was busy buttering his bread, he lifted the lid of the sugar bowl a little way and let it drop with a loud clatter, again and again, with shorter and shorter intervals.

"Stop that, I tell you." She snatched the lid from him and pushed the sugar bowl out of his reach.

He pouted sulkily and slumped back in his chair, ignoring his plate. Then he lunged forward and grabbed the milk jug, holding it at such a steep angle that the milk spilled from the lip on to the tablecloth.

"You wicked boy." She gave him a smart rap over the knuckles.

He hit back immediately.

She was too astonished to speak. Her hand glanced off his temple. His head juddered sideways. He squirmed on his chair and started kicking the leg of the table non-stop.

The Aunts tried not to notice. They emptied their cups and folded up their napkins. The only sign of annoyance as far as I could make out was Aunt Odette's eyebrow shooting up. She must have been seething with disapproval.

Unlike Flora and Alice, who were always telling me to be quiet and behave myself, and whose clips on the ear were more like caresses, Aunt Odette bottled up her anger. When I was making a nuisance of myself and wouldn't listen, she would sometimes grab me by the back of the neck, sinking a fingernail into the skin like a sting. She didn't join in the "carambas" of the others when I played bullfighter to my father's bull, chivalrously dropping to my knees after the coup de grâce to hug him and staunch his wounds.

She sipped her drink, never gulped it down. In the evening she would sit on the bench under the rose bush with her eyes closed, soaking up the light of the setting sun, as if she possessed no warmth of her own and had to seek it elsewhere.

On my wanderings through the house I sometimes came upon her unexpectedly in the vicinity of the cellar or in the larder, where sausages and rashers were kept on the highest shelves, well out of my reach. Why she furtively scooped spoonfuls of butter, or trickled coffee beans into a box with deft, practised fingers, was a mystery to me. She counted the number of scoops, and listened attentively to the beans hitting the bottom of the box as if they were just as valuable as the coins in her soft leather purse, which I was permitted to hold occasionally, but never to open.

I was equally mystified as to why, back in her room, she stored away her prizes, adding butter to butter and coffee to coffee or pouring sugar from a scrap of paper twisted into a cone on top of the sugar she already possessed.

It was as though she could not abide depletion of any kind. The drawers of her wardrobe emitted a permanent aroma of roasted coffee beans, crystalised fruit and chocolate. The smoky scent of sliced ham suggested a state of overabundance that would never end. Perhaps, like me, she was overcome with an inexplicable sadness at the sight of anything becoming less than it was before. The jam jar, which, after each breakfast, had less and less jam in it and more and more unpardonable emptiness. The dismal sight of empty preserving jars and bottles on the shelves in the cellar, their mouths agape in a rictus of thirst.

The same sadness spread through me now as I contemplated the table before me. The beaker of milk, still generous and full. The plate with the sliced bread, not as yet chewed by my teeth, the promise they held intact.

Perhaps Aunt Odette understood only too well what was holding me back. Thrilled and subdued by the thought of the sheer plenty, of all that food having to vanish without trace, I clutched a slice of bread in both fists without taking a single bite. I didn't care if Roland was giving me scornful looks.

"You're dawdling again, I do believe," my mother sighed. She pulled the bread from my hands. "I haven't got all day."

She fed me my sandwich at top speed, barely allowing me the time to swallow. Then she reached for my beaker of milk and tilted it firmly against my mouth. I struggled to push the beaker away, and the milk nearly went up my nose.

I gasped for breath and glanced around the room, smacking my lips.

"The lad's such a slow eater," one of the Aunts said.

"He's in a dream," said Aunt Odette, "the image of his father at that age. He used to sit and stare at his food just like that."

My stomach began to rumble loudly, and a sudden cramp convulsed my gut. I gave a little moan.

All eyes turned to me.

"Something coming? Ah, something coming, is that it?" giggled Aunt Alice. Roland was grinning too.

I went red in the face. Blood rushed to my cheeks and my stomach went rock-hard. Inside my body it was as though lids were relentlessly being screwed and unscrewed to seal certain ducts and open others.

I couldn't breathe, and when the twinges of pain shifted from my stomach downwards, there to burst through a thousand membranes, I felt quite dizzy.

"Go on, well done," the Aunts chirped.

Roland's mother smiled. "Look at the poor lamb struggling."

A sigh of relief escaped me. A fresh coolness spread across my cheeks, and I felt so light all of a sudden I was almost lifted right out of my chair.

"There's a clever boy!" The Aunts clapped their hands.

On other days I would have joined them in their jubilation. I might also have banged my beaker on the table and cheered loudly, but today I was discouraged by Roland's sniggers.

When my mother pulled the pot out from under me and a rush of startlingly cool air brushed my bottom, I was close to tears.

For all his mother's admonitions to be quiet and sit still and to mind his manners for goodness' sake, Roland went on hooting with laughter.

From the stairs came a bellowing man's voice, "That's enough!"

Uncle Roger burst into the room, strode up to Roland and slapped him so hard that a blood-red weal appeared on his cheek.

For a second Roland held my gaze. He was speechless, wounded to the quick, and his face went scarlet. Then he scrambled down from his chair and bolted into the corridor, sobbing.

His mother made to get up from the table.

"Let him be," said Uncle Roger. He tightened the buckle of his belt. "That boy will be the death of us."

He sat down and poured himself a cup of coffee. Leaning forward to reach for the bread basket, his attention was caught by me.

His face cleared. "So, and how is our little lad?" he asked. "Everything all right then?" And he winked at me.

I winked back at him, with both eyes at the same time. My lips budded out.

CHAPTER 3

Having a bath with my father was infinitely preferable to having one with my mother. With her everything had to be done quickly, no messing about. First she stood me in the empty tub to soap me up from head to toe, then she soaped herself. She didn't seem to care that the cold was chiselling me out of the warm air and the soap was pricking viciously my eyes.

When I huddled against her legs for protection my fingers strayed across the stretch marks on her lower abdomen, feeling the vertical grooves on either side of her navel. I had seen her stand in front of the mirror, pinching the slack skin between her fingers with a little sigh, as if I had caused her body to split down the middle when she gave birth.

How different her sex was, compared to mine and my father's, which were like spouts with a knobby lid at the end. Hers seemed to be hiding in its own folds. Past the big bush of hair, it lay curled up like a frightened hedgehog in the shrubbery. When she leaned back to soap her buttocks the strange ridge pouted into view, sliding out from its hiding place between her thighs and quickly back again.

She turned on the tap even more brusquely than other mornings. The warm water restored me to the world of warmth and comfort and my eyes stopped prickling.

A faint smile crossed her face when I shrieked with pleasure, but she had no patience for my delight as I clawed the gush of water and squeezed the sponge to make it pour.

She always had dark rings under her eyes. Her chronic fatigue gave her face the look of the finest, most fragile porcelain, but in fact she was tough. She shelled peas, made the beds. Day after day she would lay the table with a loud clatter so the whole house could hear. With each portion of overcooked vegetables she dished out she was proclaiming her domestic pride—to us of course, but especially to the Aunts. Reminding them that it was she who prepared the bean soup, she who kept their blood pressure down by baking salt-free bread especially for them; indeed that it was she who provided the four meals a day upon which their idle lives depended.

"She has no idea," the Aunts grumbled behind their napkins. "Too hoity-toity she is. Never got her hands dirty either. Never dealt with a farrowing sow."

My mother towelled me dry, dragged the collar of my shirt over my too-large head, pulled my arms through the sleeves, clicked my braces on to my trousers and tried to stuff my feet into my slippers.

"Don't curl your toes like that," she sighed crossly, "or it'll take all day."

She let me step into my slippers myself and then brushed my hair into a quiff, even though she knew I didn't like it.

"You can stay upstairs for a bit, with Aunt Odette." She put me down on the floor. "Downstairs you'd just get in the way."

I had never seen Aunt Odette looking so stately, all in black. Cascades of pleats enveloped her skinny frame and she smelled even older than she was. Even dustier. Even drier.

"She's the sort that snuffs out like a candle," my father used to say. "The sort you come upon all stiff in a chair, like a dead crow on a branch."

She had spread an old bedcover on the floor and tipped the building blocks on top.

"Why don't you build me a fine tower," she said sweetly, but her smile betrayed impatience. I knew she wanted to have done with me.

She took up one of her old photo albums and began to turn the stiff cardboard pages, and the tissue paper separating them made a soft, pattering sound like raindrops, making me glad to be with her in spite of her aloofness. Aunt Odette rarely addressed me directly, unless I needed chiding, and even then she preferred summoning my father as if he were her servant, but she made strange secret sounds, which intrigued me like the words of a foreign language.

I set about creating the tallest tower I had ever built, merely for the reward of her feigned amazement. Then, out of the corner of my eye, I saw her rise quickly to rummage in the dark wooden cabinet. Thinking she was unobserved, she carefully unwrapped a ruby-red boiled sweet and popped it into her mouth with a practised air, as though it were an extra-large indigestion tablet.

I felt my cheeks burn with indignation. Once she was seated again I heard the click of the sugary gem against her molars. Her lips parted from time to time to emit soft sucking sounds. Soon I was drooling so profusely that my saliva tasted almost as sweet as the real thing.

Aunt Odette breathed serene contentment. Now and then odd-sounding words passed her lips. She was so engrossed in her photographs that she seemed to be in a blissful dream, in the middle of which she sighed and said, with a rare tremor of ecstasy in her voice, "Yugoslavia," or "Prague. Such a lovely city. *Praha*, they call it."

Fired by her emotion, I shouted "*Praha*" in response, accidentally knocking down my tower, at which she gave me a look of affectionate surprise and ruffled my hair with her bony fingers.

"Yes," she laughed. "*Praha. Praha* is a thousand times lovelier than Vienna."

I waited for her to doze off. She had already slipped off her shoes and put her legs up on the sofa with a great swish of petticoats, and propped a cushion in the small of her back.

Downstairs was busy. I could make out the tinkle of spoons against teacups and the occasional dull pop of a cork bursting from a bottle-neck.

After a while the noise died away. Aunt Odette had already shut her album. Now her chin sank on to her breast. I got up.

*

The door gave willingly when, standing on tiptoe, I twisted the handle. There was no teasing little whinge as it swung open.

Of all the doors in the house there were some that colluded with me when I ventured on forbidden forays, and there were others that gave a tell-tale creak as they fell to behind me. There were drawers that responded eagerly when pulled open, as though jumping at the chance, and other obstinate ones that resisted or jammed halfway or refused to budge once they were sticking all the way out like gaping jaws, no matter how hard I tugged. Hidden inside them were entire worlds, compact universes, held together by a logic or gravity that eluded me. Bits of string tangled up with locks of snipped-off hair. Lame-fingered gloves clawing at frayed collars, perhaps in search of their other half. Loose cuff links. A scattering of stamps, some unused and others heavily postmarked, but all of them yellowed.

How many more treasures were there, hidden away in all the drawers I couldn't reach? What could be housed on the summits of the storage cupboards? Some of them went all the way up to the ceiling. Even when my father carried me aloft, their contents remained unseen. There were bound to be far more exciting panoramas to observe than the same old rows of plates and glassware that came within my field of vision.

I was on the landing, and it was oddly quiet in the house. Out in the yard voices tailed away. Outside the window at the end of the corridor, the crown of the nut tree burst into flames in the dying sun. In the kitchen someone filled a bucket of water and shut the back door.

From my parents' room came the sound of my father talking in a low voice to my mother. He had left his shoes by the door. I picked them up, carried them to the middle of the corridor, sank down on the wooden floor and kicked off my slippers.

I placed the shoes side by side. A smidgen of my father's warmth still lingered inside, a hint of his sweat, when I stepped shakily into his shoes. An odd sort of tremor ran up my calves, as though the strength of his legs were seeping up from the soles into my own muscles. I had a sense of stepping lightly, of being four times as tall, although in reality I advanced with difficulty, dragging my feet. It was time for everything to wake up again.

The objects in the house showed themselves to their best advantage only to people who were bigger than me. Anyone as small as me, puny even in my father's shoes, had to make do with a view seen from a low, distorting angle. The ghastly loops of dusty cobwebs between cupboard and wall or under the sink, in which dead flies with devoutly folded legs quivered in the draught. Or the toad that showed up on the back doorstep every night, crawling into the strip of bright light under the door and clearing its throat repeatedly, as if it had a weighty message to deliver. There were the spiders, whose rightful home was out in the pine trees by the chicken run. In the annexe at the back of the house, among rusty milk churns and watering cans, they had spun webs like pointed caps blown off magicians' heads, from which they emerged in a flash whenever a prey announced itself.

I liked the place best of all in the hours before supper, when everything went quiet and the house draped its walls comfortably about my shoulders. Whenever I ventured into one of the rooms, or when I was in my father's shoes zigzagging down the corridor, past all the doors behind which I caught the muffled sounds of the small habits in which everyone indulged, it was as though the space that enfolded the house seemed to divide like a cell and keep on doubling, again and again, until there was no end to it and time vanished into an infinity of folds.

The spare rooms at the back of the house, which were normally empty and bare except for the elaborate crocheted counterpanes on the beds that reminded me of the Aunts when they dressed up for special occasions, were now full of suitcases. The wardrobe doors were open, and inside I saw coats and suits which carried the scent of other houses in their seams. There were shoes scattered around the legs of the bedside tables, on top of which lay white handkerchiefs or piles of folded newspapers crowned by spectacles in awesome frames.

The brass locks of the suitcases shone seductively. How I wished I could reach them on those high forbidding beds, if only to hear the cold mechanical click as they sprung open.

*

In the last room, at the very end of the passage, I came upon a huge black coat lying on a sofa. It hung over the bolstered arm, with part of the front turned back, as though a sturdy lady's calf might emerge from it any moment. The collar of dark fur glistened so invitingly that it was impossible to resist.

I sank down on my haunches and leaned forward in my father's shoes at a perilous angle to bury my cheeks, nose and forehead in the soft tickle of myriad hairs. The satin lining smelt sweet in a dry sort of way, and felt like cool water under the flat of my hand.

I was on the point of letting myself fall face down on the coat so as to lose myself altogether in the blissful, caressing sensation when I heard footsteps. Their jaunty pace did not bode well.

I froze, pulled the flap of the coat over my head and wondered what would happen next. The footsteps halted.

The satin was absorbing my body heat fast, and the steam from my breath couldn't escape. When I stuck my head out for a breath of air, I found myself looking straight into my cousin Roland's mischievous face.

"Down in the hole. Down in the hole," he intoned, tapping each of my shoulders several times with his forefinger. "Down in the hole."

I was desperate to get away. The mere thought of the torture he had inflicted on me a few hours earlier was enough to make my eyes sting with tears.

He skipped across the room and stood in the doorway, all bright and shiny, as neat as he had been at breakfast, except for his trousers, which were streaked with chalk and bits of cobweb. He must have been snooping around the whole house, all the remotest outposts of my very own castle.

The chalk on his thighs could only have come from the walls in the cellar, the one place I had never dared to explore all by myself, where it always smelled of damp and mould and where the weak light bulb flickered as scarily as a candle that might blow out any moment. In winter the ground water oozed up between the tiles, leaving little bumps of salt behind when it dried, as white as the powdery snow that drifted into the attic through the chinks between the roof tiles. The attic and the cellar were the only parts of the house that were not sealed off from the outside world, a condition I found both appealing and daunting.

"Have a look. Come on," Roland whispered. He was leaning with one shoulder against the door frame, picking at a bit of dead skin around the thumbnail of one hand until he drew blood.

For a second I thought I was supposed to admire him for bleeding, that he took pleasure in administering pain to himself as brutally as to me or his mother. But he raised his thumb to his mouth and licked the wound.

"Come on!" he urged, grabbing me roughly by the arm when I hesitated.

He set off at a brisk pace. I could barely keep up with him. My father's shoes flew off my feet, tumbled over the floor and bounced against the skirting board. I felt like screaming, shouting that he shouldn't go so fast, but I restrained myself. I didn't want to wake Aunt Odette or alarm my father.

We stumbled down the stairs, through the passage, round the corner, past the grandfather clock, to the annexe. I had been there often enough, but now I was wandering in a foreign place. It didn't feel right that I was being led, like a visitor, a stranger, but Roland wouldn't let go of my hand.

He slowed down and stopped in front of a closed door. I knew it well, even though the glass panel was a shield of darkness rather than glowing with the familiar light of the window beyond.

Roland twisted the handle and swung the door wide open.

An unfamiliar chill struck my face. Air that felt unexpectedly fresh, without the merest hint of snuff or pipe tobacco, nor of booze or men fast asleep.

Roland pushed me into the room. It was pitch dark. I only knew where I was when the cold floor underfoot made way for the thick pile of a carpet. Behind me I could hear Roland fumbling along the walls. Something clicked under his fingers and the light went on.

Michel was lying on the bed, motionless in his best suit, eyebrows raised. Even though his eyes were shut I had the feeling he was surprised to see me there, or that he was pretending to be annoyed because I had the cheek to disturb him.

The line of his lips curved up at one corner of his mouth and down at the other, half-smile and half-scowl, as though he couldn't make up his mind whether to make me hoot with laughter or cry out in fear. His hands were yellow, his nails blue.

The pillow supporting his astonishingly bald head—I had rarely seen him without his cap—was decked with twigs of cherry laurel, and at his feet lay a bouquet of early dahlias.

For all I knew he was tricking me. At harvest time, in the barn, he pretended he was the corn monster, and in the orchard he would give the almond tree a sudden shake when I passed, unsuspecting, underneath.

"Michel," I called out, half-grinning.

"Shshsh," Roland whispered. He clapped a sweaty hand over my mouth.

I drew back indignantly.

"Michel!" I cried again.

Roland brushed past me and stopped a few paces short of the bed. He tucked his hands under his arms, as if he too expected Michel would leap up any minute and chase us down the passage to tap us on the backside with his walking stick.

He did not move.

Roland went up to the bed and slouched against the mattress. He extended his arm and covered Michel's hand with his.

My heart lurched, but aside from an almost inaudible click of the rosary beads in the blue fingers, nothing happened.

Roland looked at me, hunching his shoulders.

"Down in the hole," he said solemnly, "down in the hole."

CHAPTER 4

N IGHT ALWAYS FELL SUDDENLY, and it was with the same suddenness that the shutters were flung open and the blinds raised in the front room, where the coffin resting on trestles shone darkly. I was swung from arm to arm, washed, brushed, given milk to drink, and when everyone was gathered in the hall my mother rounded on my father, exclaiming, "Pa, what have you done? I did say to put on his black shoes, not the pale ones."

The house had filled up over the past few days. In the front room and in the kitchen I'd had to squeeze through hedges of shins and calves to get anywhere near my father or my mother. She was standing by the sink, sweating as she turned the handle of the meat grinder. Women I had never seen before were watching her every move. They addressed me as "Antoine".

The night before I had listened as everyone trooped through the house, all the way to Michel's room. I had stood up in my cot and leaned against the raised side, straining to hear.

I heard Roland tiptoe across the landing to the stairs. He sat down on the top step and I caught the sound of him scratching the paint off the skirting board.

They must have been praying, but I thought they were singing or reciting poems about rosebuds in the rain.

For the past few days I had taken to slipping away, when the others were still at table, to open the door of Michel's room and check whether he was awake and moving yet. But he had ignored me each time.

I had shown him my new toy car, and the kite that hadn't been torn to shreds in the branches of the beech tree, and my orange tin box; but even my silver spoon, which was shinier than anything I had ever seen, had not been enough to provoke a reaction. In the end I just stayed away and sulked. Quite soon I hardly knew he was there.

*

We advanced like shadows over the dyke road. Hunched shoulders. Furry collars. Black leather. Veils. I was the only one wearing pale shoes.

Around us everything glittered and made us blink. The bleached corn leaned sideways in swathes. The parched poplar foliage, already curling at the edges, rustled crisply overhead, and the grey ostrich plumes on the hearse bobbed up and down, as comically as the pompons on the ponies' bridles when the circus came to town and the clown's trousers fell down.

My father swung me over the potholes by one arm. Every few steps my mother raised her hand to massage her ear lobe between thumb and forefinger or to pat the lapels of her coat.

Now and then I caught a glimpse of Roland a few paces ahead of me, wedged between his parents. He was being propelled forward rather than walking in step, and several times I saw his feet kicking in mid-air above the cobbles.

As she passed, Aunt Odette gave my shoulder a squeeze with a black-gloved hand that reminded me of a bird's scaly claw. She hissed that I was to behave myself, later on.

"Listen!" she said, pointing her finger to her ear. "The bells, already…"

I heard the slow tolling of the bell and the long silences between each stroke, and I was overcome with boredom. Everything clotted together in the heat.

*

The rooms where the grown-ups gathered to while away their boredom were places that spelled boredom for me. In the café on Sundays after Mass the rattling of dice, the grunts and cries from a dart thrower and the thumping of fistfuls of cards on table-tops mingled in a heaving swell of tedium on which I floated, feeling seasick. I would clutch the legs of a bar stool for support, or my father's legs as he stood drinking and laughing.

There was the mild boredom of the women as they sat on the chairs they had taken outside, with their skirts hitched up over their knees. Bent on catching the last rays of sunlight, they craned their necks and spoke little, and for a moment that lasted for ever they manifested the same inanimate truculence as my rag dolls and my bears, on those intensely monotonous days when everything seemed to defy my imagination.

Boredom also nestled in the lofts over the stables, where years of undisturbed compaction had transformed it into bales of straw more akin to dust, and in the boxes containing rusty forks and spoons under my father's work bench. A mere glimpse of them was enough to make me feel as lost and abandoned as the tarnished cutlery itself, which left a sour aftertaste on your fingertips if you touched them.

Deadliest of all, though, was the boredom of church, where the vaulted ceilings held every second captive and the priest, like a puppet attached to invisible strings, knelt jerkily, broke bread and drank wine without offering me a taste.

A man with a gold tooth in the corner of his mouth and a peaked cap had awaited us in the portal. After the coffin had been lifted from the hearse, he separated the men from the women with a casual gesture.

My father sat me on the chair beside him and pressed a soft toy into my hands. Roland was sitting in the row behind us, rocking agitatedly from side to side. Now and then he glanced up at his father to see how he was coping with the enervation.

Cymbals clanged. My father turned our seats and knelt on the prayer stool. I sat down on mine with my back to the altar.

Roland reached for the tips of my shoes, and in doing so dropped a handful of coins, which skittered across the floor.

"Pick them up," his father hissed.

Roland cowered. He was out of his element, a world with nooks and crannies for hiding in, a place where he could calculate distances and escape routes, like this morning, when he had plunged in among the coats hanging from the pegs as soon as his mother came near. She was sitting across the aisle, on the other side of the bier, and sank down on her knees so devoutly as to elicit a faint smile from Aunt Odette. When the priest sent the collection box round, she drew from her handbag a tight roll of bills which crackled softly but had more impact than the brassy jingle of the coins donated by the other Aunts.

Even in church, under the heaven-high arches, she was like an elephant absorbing all the space around her and elbowing everyone who came near into a corner. Roland must have plopped out of her body without leaving any trace at all, or only the most fleeting ripple. He must have escaped her like an unwelcome thought, an unforeseen, unpleasant surprise which had left her daydreams in tatters and had been twisting doorknobs and knocking over vases ever since.

On the flagstones at my feet I followed the wavy calcite patterns like the courses of rivers on a map, until they ended at the mortar-filled edge. All around me the stained glass windows of the south apse dissolved into patches of colour. Time waded through sand.

It puzzled me that grown-ups should want always to sit still, not to move at all or hardly, and ended up stowing themselves away in a box with a lid on top, to be dead and gone.

When the priest walked round the coffin sprinkling holy water we got wet, too, and I pulled the hood of my jacket over my head without thinking. My father slipped it down again with a smile.

"Just hang on a little bit longer," he said. "It'll all be over soon."

*

In the mound of fresh earth beside the yawning hole among the gravestones, I glimpsed fat, shiny earthworms poking out briefly before wriggling back in. Roland held tight to his father's hand and peered cautiously over the side. Clods of earth thudded on to the wood.

Two nights earlier, my father had woken me up in the

middle of the night. He had taken me in his arms and carried me downstairs. To my mother's protests he had replied, "It's all right for him to see."

We had stood around the foot of the coffin. Beside me the Aunts sent their rosaries flying through their fingers.

Roland's father supported the old man's head while the trunk and the legs were lifted up by two others. Wearing the same expression of mockery mixed with scorn, Michel had allowed them to lower him into the casket.

It was only when the Aunts kissed his forehead one by one that for a moment I had the impression his eyes had opened a crack. All of a sudden he had seemed angry, stricken by a stubborn fury, the way I sometimes felt when my mother hid my building blocks from me and I held my breath in outrage.

My father leaned across to lay his hand on Michel's forehead, just before the lid was closed. He had put my hand on Michel's forehead.

"Cold," I had said.

My mother fled into the garden.

*

"Down in the hole," Roland sang. His mother clapped her hand over his mouth and jerked him back, into the crowd.

A while later I saw him saunter out of the churchyard, past the wrought iron gate. His father swore under his breath but did not go after him.

Somewhere a dog barked, and almost at once Roland reappeared, ashen-faced and hurrying up the path. He'd got a fright, which pleased me.

His father turned round. "Come here," he said, extending an arm.

Roland bent down.

The gravediggers thrust their spades into the earth.

"Why don't you walk with us," Aunt Alice said.

My father had his arm round my mother's waist. People shuffled past, men doffed their hats, my father nodded.

No-one spoke. The heat was oppressive.

"One metre seventy," Flora said. "I thought he was shorter."

Aunt Odette unclasped her handbag and stuffed her handkerchief inside.

"They always look smaller when they're dead."

*

Out in the yard, under the beech tree, folding tables were set up, glasses were filled to the brim and trays piled high with sandwiches were handed round. As soon as we got back, Roland's mother had gone upstairs to change her dark clothes for a salmon-pink frock. The Aunts were scandalised.

"Sometimes it's more sudden than you think," Roland's father said. "Myself, I'd want to make sure I was in a decent state before I died. Someone's always got to clean up the mess."

"Diddle diddle doo," sang Aunt Flora, her cheeks wobbling as she bounced me on her knee.

"Was I happy when you came along! Sooo happy! Corneel and I only produced girls, and Aunt Odette, poor thing, she never even got hitched. Far too picky, she was. No-one was good enough. Too fat, too thin, too rich, too poor."

She raised her glass of port wine to my lips.

45

"There, have a sip," she urged quietly when no-one was looking, and again, and again, until the world reeled and swayed as I slithered down her shins.

*

It was one of those summer days when flying ants swarmed up from their nests en masse to dance over the treetops, and swallows scissored through the swarms.

"Anton, d'you want a sandwich?" my mother cried, but I did not reply.

I wandered off towards the stone steps leading to the vegetable patch and the fence where the woodbine crept up to invade the boughs of the beech tree.

I wanted to play in the orchard or by the vegetable patch, or in the lee of the hedges, where at this time of year the windless afternoon air vibrated minutely as a peach dropped from a tree and bounced two or three times on the tufted grass. I wanted to see how the stoneweed growing in the cracks between the paving stones folded its halo of fleshy leaves against the sun, and to hear the leisurely flap-flap of hens unfurling their wings like fans.

I wanted to follow the sandy path to the end of the orchard and thread my arm carefully through the thorny sprays of bramble to pick the first blackberries, all the way at the back, where the unknown vastness began.

The plum tree had shed a few early, unripe fruit, which lay fermenting in the grass. Soon they would burst, and clouds of buzzing flies or wasps would settle on them to gobble them up. Afterwards, the leftover stones would bleach in the grass.

There was a weeping willow by the old ice-house next to the pond which had been dug long ago, before Belgium came into existence, but which had been filled in since. My father leaned against the trunk and said, "Look, that's where we'd hide when the bombers came over, in that dark hole over there. We slept on straw, like rabbits. Remember, Roger?"

Uncle Roger nodded. "Our father used to say there's no safer roof than the roots of a tree. They hold the stones in place. Still, he did cross himself when they bombed the bridge. The pieces flew right over the shed."

"We were lucky," my father said. "Damned lucky. You don't realise when you're young. I thought it was exciting. Better than fireworks."

"And in the winter of forty-one," Uncle Roger said, "we used to cross the frozen canal to get to school. Ma was furious. Yet the ice was at least half a metre thick."

"She was always worrying. It's not until you have kids of your own that you can see why." My father took his hands out of his trouser pockets, took a deep breath, gave me a poke and cried, "Race you to the bottom!"

I charged down the slope, stumbling over the tussocky grass.

He gave me a head start. "Watch out. There's an ugly monster chasing you," he cried.

Over my shoulder I saw Uncle Roger crawling towards me on all fours, teeth bared and growling alarmingly.

"A great big dog," my father chuckled. "He's going to bite you in the bum."

My foot shot into a hole and I fell flat on my face.

Two hands grabbed me under my arms and pulled me upright. Uncle Roger put his teeth against my neck, my tummy, and swung me round by my arms.

Air whooshing past my ears. Tingle in the stomach.

"Fatty, fatty, fatty, you're a Swiss cheese patty." He put me down.

I fell over backwards.

Treetops, roofs, clouds wheeled around me. I could hear the Aunts taking the dishes into the kitchen, chairs being folded with a clatter.

My father knelt on the grass beside me. It was summer. Branches drooping with foliage and a blue-and-white sky beyond.

I ran my hands over his bare forearms.

"Fatty, fatty, like a Swiss cheese patty." He flung a handful of grass in my face.

I blew the blades away, groped for his neck, and the world broke into smithereens of sheer delight.

PART II

CHAPTER I

GOING ON FOR TWELVE, and unfulfilled. I outgrew all my shirts in the twinkling of an eye. The world that had surrounded me so fondly up till then was beginning to resemble ancient wallpaper that might come unstuck any minute. The wardrobe mirrors still reflected robust beds with crucifixes beneath the light switch. All those Saviours fashioned out of copper or porcelain, or plated with pewter, all of them nailed and writhing. In the room that once belonged to Alice the palm frond still smelt faintly of the scent she had taken to sprinkling on it once she discovered that holy water was nothing but tap water that had been blessed by a priest.

The world had grown brittle, as friable as an Egyptian mummy or a desiccated chrysalis deep in the bark of a tree. A clap of thunder would be enough to pulverise it. In summer the stands of poplar trees managed to screen the chimney stacks of the new industrial estate, but in winter the stark factory halls edged the sunlight with the chill blink of aluminium. And although my father had planted a new hedge to hide where part of the garden and the fields beyond had been bulldozed away, the high green wall did not stop the rumble of trucks on the new elevated bridge from carrying right over the stables and pouring into the yard.

On the horizon cars raced over roads that hadn't been there before.

The sodium lighting along the brand-new motorway cast an orange glow in the night. A few years back, on a grey day in late autumn, the mayors of the neighbouring communities had held a joint ceremony to open the new approach road. Standing shoulder to shoulder they had snipped the tricolour ribbon, eliciting a little burst of applause from the crowd. There was a picture in the local newspaper: in among the ladies' hats and freshly sculpted hairdos were my father and Uncle Roger, both wearing expressions of mild scorn. They stood on either side of Roland's mother, whose lips shaped the O of bravo, looking up as the reporter clicked the shutter.

Stuyvenberghe, our home town, was now linked to modernity for good. We were to reap the bittersweet harvest in time, but for now the brass band stood poised in readiness in the background and the church square became a temporary fairground.

*

"The Callewijn family's like an old shrub," my father used to say. "Plenty of young shoots in the old days, all but withered now." He'd have liked ten children. Ten bedrocks in which to lay his sorrow to rest, without ever abandoning his unrealised hopes for me and my unborn brothers and sisters. He had dreamed of taking up a technical profession, of being a civil engineer. It would have been him running the construction site that was rising all around us, putting up new illusions and demolishing old ones. By the age of ten he was already making technical drawings of imaginary machines. Gears and cog wheels. Complicated engines. Infinitely complex pumping installations which transported his dreams and eventually, when he was seventeen, sent them up in smoke. His father fell ill. Six weeks after the tests one of his legs was amputated. Not long after that the other one followed. It was in his lungs, too. He died a year later. The fields were leased and most of the cattle sold off. Someone had to be the breadwinner, and as Uncle Roger had already been studying for rather a long time, my grandmother, with characteristic pre-war fatalism, must have decided that taking her youngest boy out of school would be less of a waste.

From then on my father came home every evening around six, covered in flour-dust from the silos at the milling plant. His job was to pour the grain into troughs and watch it rattling over the conveyor belt before it vanished into machines that had not been designed by him.

But I remained an only child, the youngest shoot on the crown of a tree that was steadily dying back. A puny eleven-year-old, my frame not strong enough to bear the full weight of the past and far from ready for the future that was gnawing at my bones. My joints swelled up, my legs grew long and spindly. During the night my muscles twanged like tight strings, sending stabs of pain through my sleep.

My voice had already broken, on a high A-note during the *bonae voluntatis* on the day of the Assumption of the Virgin Mary, in the twilight of the rood-loft. Mr Snellaert, the choir master, who used to go all dewy-eyed at the high reach of my chorister voice, had firmly banished me to the back row with the altos, where I was put next to a girl named Roswita. She had a high forehead in a triangular face and a bosom that had surged into womanhood way ahead of the rest of her.

She still wasn't used to wearing a bra, and the straps bothered her. Reins, she called them. They kept slipping down her shoulders, at which she would slide her hand into her blouse or jumper to adjust them with a sigh that suggested as much pride as annoyance.

At night, when she shed her flimsy dress in her bedroom, the red marks on her shoulders left by the straps would be like the welts on the Aunts' thighs when they took off their boned corsets or garter belts—but she wasn't anywhere near as fleshy as Flora, who, before she got cancer, would wake up in the morning to find that the sheets had carved veritable canyons into her buttocks, which took ages to disappear.

It was only a matter of time before girls burgeoned into women, layered with sleekness and soft bumps. What time did to me was wreak havoc with old established ties and rudely rearrange the loose ends inside my body. Those were the years when I would grind my teeth and go into a sulk for days without knowing why.

I needed everything else to change, too, irreparably so. The doors of my toy cars had to rattle on their hinges when I raced them over the uneven floor tiles. Sand from the sandpit would have to clog up the axles, they'd have to lose their wheels, which would go skittering across the floorboards and down the stairs, where they would be subsumed into an orgy of discards at the bottom. I had picked at the seams in the sides of my teddy bears until they gave way, had stuck my fingers inside to grope for hearts and livers. Even my building blocks, so irritatingly solid despite the growth rings of the tree on the outside, were put to the test by my attempting to sink my teeth into them.

"You don't deserve such nice toys," my mother groused when she saw the slaughter of arms and legs around my bed, the splayed hands with dented fingertips, the dismembered bodies and severed heads, empty and gaping like the discarded mantle of a reptile or an insect.

She used to buy my clothes a size or two too big, so I could grow into them. My shirts flapped draughtily around my ribcage, and I had to secure my trousers with a belt to keep them in place.

"You wear stuff out faster than your Dad earns his wages. Money doesn't grow on trees, you know."

She was always hearing about obscure warehouses with cut-price sales, where plenty of clothing and shoes could be picked up for half the normal price. She would order my father to get into the car and push me on to the back seat, after which she would rummage through the profusion of notes, shopping lists and receipts in her pockets for the scrap of paper with directions that a neighbour or distant cousin had spelled out for her.

"Best if we take the side roads," she would instruct, as if the straight lines of the motorway were offensive to the meanderings of her mental landscape.

My father had given up protesting. He had even stopped letting out a sigh of resignation before turning the key in the ignition. Even if we were completely lost within the hour, bumping over twisting country roads, with my mother in the front beside him staring agitatedly at the creased scrap of paper in her fingers, and then out the window again in the hope of spotting a phone box with a plastic rubbish bin next to it, a front garden with azaleas, or the chip shop where we were supposed to make a left turn, or a right and then over the railway crossing—the effect on my father was always the same: his exasperation was transformed into a veneer of cool detachment which seemed to cover the windows on the inside with a mist of ice crystals.

Now and then he glanced in the rear-view mirror. His eyes met mine in a look of complicity.

Our destination would invariably be some derelict factory hall in the ragged outskirts of the city. The walls showed signs of old advertisement hoardings having been removed and replaced by hastily painted placards shouting "Lido" or "Textima", the names of shady businesses which sprouted like poppies on wasteland only to shrivel almost immediately. The bleak euphoria of slogans like *Rock-Bottom Prices*, *Everything Must Go*, or *Your Savings Paradise*, made my mother quicken her pace.

Inside, in the glow of neon strip lights, half of which were blinking nervously, was a scene of mass plunder. Women trailing husbands and children in exactly the same state of bored resignation as my father and myself plunged their arms into troughs full of clothing. Holding their bunches of socks or underwear jammed under their elbows, they were like bumble bees weighed down with pollen as they descended on one heap after another, savouring, clawing, groping.

She made me try everything on. If there weren't fitting rooms I would have to take my clothes off in front of everybody, no matter how loudly I protested.

"Don't be so silly," my mother would cry. "Nobody's looking. Anyway, there's no hair between your legs yet."

Actually, I had cut off the first four hairs out of sheer astonishment at what I saw in the mirror in my room, as though nature had decided to furnish my groin with whiskers, a goatee in the wrong place. For weeks the stubble had irritated my thighs. I had shaved them off with my father's razor, and had cauterised the cuts with eau de Cologne. After that I had given up.

If I held back long enough I knew my mother would eventually open her raincoat and hold out the sides like tent-flaps to shield me, which gave some measure of protection although it only deepened my mortification. I felt like an overgrown kangaroo joey, too small for the world, too big for the pouch. At these moments I would seek reassurance from my father, always in vain, for he would have turned away from the embarrassing spectacle, and not until it was all over would he console me with a pat on the back.

In the end the clothes found their way into my wardrobe, where the folded piles slowly absorbed the scent of my mother's trademark lavender soap. It was an act of rebellion against her compulsive tidiness—which I certainly didn't want to have passed down to me—that I clogged up my room with crumpled sheets of paper, piles of books, empty glasses, dirty clothes. I would exult in my quiet mutiny when she padded down the corridor early in the morning and I could almost hear her outrage clawing at my door as she went past.

It was only a matter of time before she could no longer resist taking action. It was usually on a Saturday, when I was having a lie-in, that she would charge into my room armed with pails, chamois leather and brushes. She would whip off my bedclothes, knowing full well how embarrassed I'd be, and regard me with barely concealed amusement as I turned over on my front as quickly as I could and groped under the bed for my underpants. Sometimes she would bend down herself to help me find them, only to retrieve the odd sock, dirty handkerchief or dusty vest, which she would hold up like a dead rat between thumb and index finger before dropping it theatrically in the laundry basket. Usually she held her tongue during these blitz operations, convinced that the noise of all the sweeping and clattering and sloshing, which pursued me to the bottom of the stairs, was the best way of conveying her disappointment in me.

*

One Saturday towards the end of August she reached boiling point. During breakfast my father and I did not speak. I kept my eyes on my plate while he glanced sideways at the newspaper lying on the table among crumbs and spots of jam. She bustled about, adjusting table settings and moving and re-moving a stack of my comics from one side table to another.

"Paradise," my father murmured to himself. He had folded the newspaper to the page with the crossword. "Four letters."

"Eden," I said.

He raised his eyebrows, lowered the tip of his ballpoint on to the paper and nodded.

I knew he knew the word without me telling him. He also knew how risky it was, with my mother hovering so close, to give the impression of being in any way pleased.

She strode towards the mantelpiece. I saw my father cringe. Woe betide him if there were any unpaid bills among the envelopes stuffed behind the clock, which she shifted ever so slightly with futile but measured precision to achieve an exact parallel with the ledge.

We ducked like schoolboys as she swept past on her way out of the room. She reappeared wearing her grey nylon apron.

"The upstairs room needs a good clean," she said curtly. "I'm not waiting till just before they arrive."

She had tied on a headscarf and knotted it under her chin, and was wearing blue galoshes. She made for the stairs bearing her brooms and long-handled mops like hatchets in the crook of her arm.

"But first I'll have a go at that pigsty of yours," she said in passing, without looking at me.

I heard her climb the stairs. She swore when a scrubbing brush slipped out of a pail and skidded down several steps.

"Why can't you clear up your own room for once?" my father asked, not expecting an answer. He got up. "We'd better start doing our bit."

*

Up in the attic there was a stack of planks covered by an old blanket, which we were to assemble into a bed.

"It's time the bed came down from up there," my mother had said several times over the past few days, in the aggrieved tone that she used in all her utterances.

We carried the planks down from the attic and left them in the room next to mine, where she was rushing around in a frenzy of tidying. She had already put my boxes containing the discarded body parts of bears and dolls by the door, so she could burn them in the back garden. I had no difficulty picturing the horror on her face as she carried the jar containing dead beetles outside, and her disgust when she found the bean plant with its roots tangled in the holes of the sponge, from which they had extracted the last drop of moisture before drying up completely.

It was my job to hold the planks level while he slid the ends into the notches in the headboard and screwed them in place.

My mother scrubbed the rusty stain in the washbasin and the spots on the mirror above until she was too exhausted to continue. She gave the writing desk, newly varnished by my father, an extra polish with her chamois and lined the shelves of the wall cabinet with dark brown paper.

It had been a few days since she had rubbed linseed oil into the floorboards. Now the heady, petrol-like smell deepened my unease at the prospect of my cousin Roland's arrival within the next few hours.

*

Had no-one ever noticed there was something peculiar about Roland's mother? With each family celebration, with each funeral her glossy furs seemed more extravagant and her cheeks more thickly streaked with powder. With each successive gathering she had grown less steady on her feet. It was as if she might collapse any moment under the weight of her gold jewellery, of which she wore increasing quantities until her neck and wrists were buried in precious stones. The more lavish her attire, the louder the note of despair in her ostentation.

I had visited their house just once. It was an immaculate villa with a scattering of ornamental rocks in the garden and a small fountain in front, where the gleam of gravel on the garden path and the Chinese vases on the window sill added to the impression of genteel grandeur. At my house they didn't mind if I came to the table with dirty hands. They didn't mind if I sailed toy boats on the slushy moat around the muck heap. I wore the smell of stables like the scent of the great outdoors, and if I tore my shirt on the holly hedge in search of blackbirds' nests I seldom got a clip around the ear, all I got was an angry look and it was over.

That afternoon found us gathered around the table like sculptures moulded to our seats, staring fixedly at the lace tablecloth and the platters with tarts that looked as if they had been modelled in clay.

Roland's mother sank her knife into the iced cake with a flourish, and when her thumb inadvertently scooped an arabesque of whipped cream she had cringed as if it were a mortal sin. She had gone to the kitchen, where she could be heard shuffling her feet and blowing her nose repeatedly. An embarrassed silence had ensued, in which the clock ticking in the hall sounded faintly sarcastic.

Roland hadn't thought of offering to show me around. He was stuck on his chair as if he were carved in stone, with his hands tucked under his thighs. When his father finally told us to be off, half the doors in the house turned out to be locked.

Through the keyholes lurked sofas with extravagantly carved legs. They were rarely sat on, and the cushions hadn't been touched since the last time someone had arranged them prettily against the back. There were books permanently cloistered behind glass, their spines pristine, untouched.

My cousin didn't have boxes with shells hidden away in his room. There wasn't a single shelf on which he kept rocks picked from the bed of a stream for the sake of their veins of gold that no-one had thought to mine.

We went into the garden. He showed me the rope ends dangling from the limb of an ailanthus tree, where his swing had been until the day he landed in the middle of mother's dahlia bed, plank and all.

We mooched among the flowerbeds edged with box and

kicked a football around half-heartedly, anxious that a poorly aimed shot might knock a Greek god off his pedestal. From the other side of the fence came the sound of girls playing in the neighbours' swimming pool. Beach balls soared like colourful enticements over the conifer hedge. Elsewhere, boys would be storming sand castles, laying ambushes and fighting lightning battles.

*

I hadn't seen much of Roland since that day, and even less of his mother. Later, when he started secondary school, there was talk of him throwing crockery around, breaking windows and stealing from shops. She had packed him off to boarding school, but he'd made such a nuisance of himself there that he'd been expelled before the year was out. Then one day, in the summer before my twelfth birthday, his father came to visit us on his own. I saw him at the kitchen table with my father, drinking gin. He sat with one of his arms hanging lamely over the back of the wooden chair, fidgeting with the frayed edge of the rush seat. His expression was as dark as a leaden sky before a hailstorm.

After he had left my father took me to the orchard.

"Roland's coming to stay with us for a while," he said. "It's for the best."

I already had a new bicycle, which I kept in the old stable. A proper bike with a big lamp powered by a dynamo which purred when I pedalled hard over the dyke in anticipation of Roland's arrival. Flying ducks skimmed my head as they swooped down to land on the water. I craned my neck to make the wind, which hugged me closer than my clothes, sing loudly in my hair.

CHAPTER 2

H is FATHER BROUGHT HIM by car. They stood facing each other forlornly in the yard. They unloaded his bike from the luggage rack, took two suitcases out of the boot, a couple of coats and a bag containing winter clothes.

"I won't come in," Uncle Roger said. "I don't like leaving Mother on her own."

Roland responded to his father's handshake with a perfunctory kiss. He followed the car as it backed out through the gate, then walked up to the dyke.

From my room I watched him amble along the towpath, kicking stones into the water. He pulled up his socks and sat down among the leafy irises on the bank. Now and then he greeted the skipper at the wheel of a passing barge with a listless wave of the hand.

He hadn't addressed a single word to me since his arrival. Before sitting down to supper that evening he made for the kitchen, unbuttoned his cuffs and held his hands under the pump. Then he took his seat at table and proceeded to cut his slice of bread into cubes, presumably because that was what they did at home.

"You'll soon settle in," my father said. "Things aren't really very different here. We're Callewijns, all of us."

He nodded briefly. He replied to all my father's questions politely, but didn't volunteer any information. Most of the time he kept his eyes on his plate.

My mother observed him with an air of concern. "Have some more milk," she said. "And do have that last meatball. It's a shame to waste it."

*

I was sent to bed an hour earlier than usual. Beneath my window I could hear my father talking to Roland. I watched them strolling amicably in the garden. My father laid his hand on Roland's shoulder a few times, and I saw him holding out his handkerchief. Roland accepted the offer and turned his back on the house, as if he knew I was spying on him.

I put on my pyjamas and lay on top of the covers, looking round my bedroom to gauge the effect of my mother's great purge and wondering whether it would arouse scorn from Roland. He was bigger than me, he wore long shorts and long socks, so that the only bits of bare leg you saw were his knees.

I considered putting up some posters of cars, maybe some of wild animals in Africa, too, so as to draw attention away from the wallpaper patterned with anthropomorphic aeroplanes wearing wide grins. I had positioned my case with its new pens for my first term at secondary school on my writing table, next to an exercise book with much-thumbed pages curling at the edges, which, I hoped, would signal seriousness and diligence. An encyclopaedia—one from the thirty-volume set my father kept in his room—lay diagonally on the table, open and with the marker ribbon trailing casually over some photos of submarines during the War.

"I'll unpack your clothes later," I heard my mother call from the kitchen, but when he came upstairs a few minutes later I could tell he was carrying his suitcases up by himself.

Oddly, he did not shut the door that connected our rooms, but left it ajar. I was pretending to be asleep so I couldn't very well get up to shut it for him.

He switched on the bedside lamp. I could hear him unzipping both suitcases, one on the table, the other on the bed. In the deepening dusk I found the sounds he was making comforting, and turned over on my side. In spite of the vague misgivings his arrival had stirred in me, I was glad I was no longer alone.

He gathered up all his socks and dumped them in the bottom drawer in one move, but for the rest of his clothing he made a separate journey each time, taking the items out of the suitcases and transferring them to the wardrobe shelves one by one. He took wire hangers from the rod and arranged his trousers on them, patting down the sharply creased legs quietly but very firmly. He must have taken his shoes off downstairs and come up in his socks, probably so as not to wake me, but the loose floorboard creaked just the same when he stepped on it.

Why he shut the doors of the wardrobe each time he had put something inside, only to have to open them again for the next item, baffled me. There was something cold and mechanical about his actions. I was reminded of the bully he used to be, how he'd go off during family get-togethers and skulk in the garden, where he'd pull the wings off butterflies and watch them drop helplessly on the path before he ground them underfoot.

Unlike me, who would occasionally amputate the antennae of a beetle or hold a moth captive between thumb and index finger for the sake of the horror I felt at its struggle to get away, the torture he inflicted seemed utterly lacking in the mercy of the true executioner. Even the constant misdeeds against his parents seemed to have more to do with unchannelled rebellious rage than with the kind of deviousness I myself was perfecting in my efforts to terrorise my mother. I had turned twelve, and needed to prove myself. A few words were enough to reduce her to tears. I played her rage as if it were a harp, and thrilled to my own beastliness.

Now she came up to Roland's room bringing soap and toilet water to put on the ledge over the washbasin. He muttered "thank you", and in the ensuing silence I knew she was sitting on his bed, next to the case, resting her hands on her knees.

I could barely make out what she was whispering, but I knew she would be saying things like, "Your mother'll be better soon. School starts the day after tomorrow. That'll take your mind off things."

I could tell by the sound of his impatient shuffling on the floorboards that he wanted her to go away. She had put him off his ritual, his strict cycles of unpacking and placing on shelves, of opening and shutting the doors of the wardrobe. He padded to and fro like a panther in a cage.

My mother slapped her thighs and said, "I'm not done yet."

The dry smack of her lips told me that he must have ducked away, so that her kiss landed on his forehead.

I don't know how long it took him to put everything away in the wardrobe. I must have dozed off. I was startled awake by the noise of something falling to the floor, a pair of shoes or an armful of books. He swore under his breath. A little later he opened the window and switched off the bedside lamp.

*

When I woke up I saw him in his pyjamas leaning against the washbasin. He was drumming his fingers on the rim while the basin filled up. He wrenched the second tap on, and jumped back when it sputtered loudly, coughing up air and gushes of rusty water.

After undressing the night before he must have put away his clothes with near-mathematical precision. The trousers were hanging neatly over the back of a chair, jumper and vest lay carefully folded on the seat, and on top of that rested a pair of socks and clean underpants.

His pyjamas received the same meticulous treatment after he took them off. He stood gazing in the mirror over the washbasin at the reflection of his chest, on which, now that he was shirtless, I spotted the first signs of hair growth.

He was a true-blue Callewijn. Tall and sinewy, dark hair, brown-black eyes. His complexion was pale, like my father's and my uncles', and seemed even to suggest a touch of anaemia, although physical exertion or strong emotions made the blood rush to his face in no time. His shoulders were covered in blemishes. The still-boyish skin was pitted with rosy craters from pimples and boils, which must have itched terribly.

As he waited for the basin to fill up, I saw his fingers crawl over his backbone. I could hear the dry scrape of his nails over his shoulder blades and his thighs, where the first tendrils of pitch-black hair clung to his buttocks.

He leaned forward, scooped water over his face with his hands and snorted in a shivery but satisfied sort of way. Taking the sponge in one hand, he soaped his armpits, the back of his neck, his chest and stomach, and with a barely perceptible shudder wiped his crotch and his buttocks. The scent of soap wafted into my room, where it collided with the air coming in through the window, bringing the smell of fresh earth and cut grass, as yet untainted by heat or dust.

He washed his feet by placing first the left foot and then the right on the edge of the basin and soaping his toes one by one. Now and then the leg he was standing on wobbled and while he regained his balance his sex dangled clumsily in the shadows beneath his buttocks.

He set about drying himself, rubbing his neck vigorously, dragging the towel across his back from side to side. He took his underpants from the chair and put them on, flexing his knees slightly to adjust his balls. Next came socks, vest and jumper, and finally he zipped up his flies and buckled his belt.

Almost done now. Time for the finale. Sitting on a chair he thrust his feet into his shoes, pulled the laces tight and made a whooshing sound as he knotted them. His shoelaces meant nothing to him, whereas I still had trouble with mine. To me they were like umbilical cords still tying me to my mother.

He rose to his feet and stared down at his shoes for a moment. Then he opened the door to the corridor, shut it quietly behind him and went down the stairs. I was alone.

*

I stepped out of bed, enjoyed the warmth of the sun on my feet and the coarse wood of the floorboards under my soles.

The elaborate morning ritual that my cousin had performed seemed unfinished, somehow, as though the energetic flapping of the towel and the speed with which he had got dressed was still generating whorls of turbulence in the air.

He was a teenager and I couldn't make him out. His room exuded a sense of order that took my breath away. There wasn't a single shoe or towel left lying around. The only thing that looked out of place lay on the bedside table, next to a little pile of books arranged according to size with the biggest one on the bottom. It was a blue-and-white handkerchief screwed up into a ball, which crackled intriguingly when I pulled it apart. The neatly made bed bore no traces of ever having been slept in, and as the window had been open the whole time, the unchaste aroma of his sleep was kept from me.

In his haste he had forgotten to pull the plug of the basin. I peered at grey soapy water with plumes of foam floating around and sticking to the sides.

I took off my pyjamas and, just as Roland had done a while ago, looked at myself in the mirror.

Slowly I began to disintegrate into the parts that came from my mother and those from my father. Her eyes, his nose. His ears, her hands. The dimple in my chin—for how many generations had it been travelling from face to face? I had seen it in photographs of my grandfather. I used to rub it with my thumb when I sat on Michel's lap, and had watched my father manoeuvre his razor around it umpteen times.

Roland didn't have one. He had the round chin of his mother, the only part of her, it seemed, that she had man-aged to smuggle into her son, aside from her sleekness, a fine layer of fat just under the skin. He was not as thin as I was. I could count my ribs and when I took a really deep breath you could almost see through my stomach to my backbone.

I felt too light, too loose-limbed for this room, where Roland had installed himself in such an orderly fashion. All his shoes in rows on the bottom of the wardrobe, his jackets in military ranks on the hangers, his shirts, with starched, manly collars, in piles on the shelves.

From the bottom of the stairs my mother called out that I'd catch it if I didn't hurry up, but I already knew I was going to be late.

Church bells rang out on the horizon. I stooped over the basin and sank my hands in the water. The sourish smell of old soap filled my nostrils. The cold made my head spin. I buried my face in the towel in which a faint smell of Roland still lingered.

CHAPTER 3

O N A CORNER of the kitchen table stood a glass of milk and a plate with half a slice of bread on it, left there by my mother. She was already waiting outside, with the others. I knew to expect a cuff on the ear, which would amount to little more than a flutter of the hands, after which she would whip out her comb to restore the side parting to my hair.

The nearer we came to the square the more churchgoers joined our party, making the patter of heels and soles on the cobbles ever louder. Wrinkled faces above snow-white collars, ankles in shiny socks peeping out from trousers that had shrunk, and on the square at the foot of the church tower everything fused into a cloud of mothballs and Woods of Windsor.

In the portal my father held the swing door open for us. My mother extended fingers moist with holy water to hold my hand and Roland's, and motioned for us to make the sign of the cross.

"We can go upstairs," I told Roland, digging him in the ribs.

He glanced up at my father, who nodded. "Go along then. You'll be less bored there."

Next to the niche where a sleepy-eyed churchwarden sat was a low wooden door. I dragged it open and started up the spiral staircase with Roland in my wake. My heart swelled with delight at the coolness rising from the stone steps and swirling round us as we wound our way up and up until the glorious moment when I gave the door of the rood-loft a little push and we stepped into the pale golden light cascading in through the window, where the chill gave way to dusty warmth.

Mr Snellaert was waiting by the keyboard. He had taken off his jacket and rolled up his shirtsleeves. The rows of chairs and benches in the space between two sets of organ pipes, a bit like a clearing in a leaden forest, were occupied by choristers flapping their song books and sheet music.

"I thought you'd overslept again," the choir master said.

"I've brought someone along. My cousin Roland."

"Roland... Roland," the choir master echoed, wrinkling his brow. "You must be Roger's boy."

Roland nodded.

"If you can sing as well as your Pa when he was a boy, you're more than welcome to join us." The choir master pressed a missal into his hands.

I threaded my way among the chairs and benches to the last row, up against the wall. Roswita was already there, wearing a grass-green blouse that strained to hold her bosom.

She was leaning forward slightly on her seat with her elbows on her knees, perhaps because she wanted to conceal her budding curves, in the midst of which a thin silver necklace quivered.

She wore quite ordinary turquoise studs in her ears, which flashed brightly when she stretched her neck with all the nonchalance she could muster and shook her mane so that everyone might admire her jewellery.

I knew I confused her by pretending not to notice, but she set me on edge, alarmed me even, with all her sighs and little groans, the hair in constant need of adjustment, the reins that kept slipping, the pleats in her skirt, her collar, the thin silver necklace, the navy-blue knee socks she wore with the sandals in which tiny pebbles got stuck, driving her crazy, so that she sometimes couldn't help shaking her feet to dislodge them. The sound of them hitting the wooden floor was magnified ten times under the vaulted ceiling.

"Move over a bit," I said. "From now on there's two of us."

She threw me an inquisitive glance as she raised her bottom off the wooden bench and lowered it further along.

"This is my cousin Roland. He's come to stay with us for a while."

Her moist eyes lit up, just as I had foreseen. The fevers raging deep inside her flared, beading her downy upper lip with perspiration.

"Where's he from?" she asked.

"You ask him," I said meanly. "He can speak for himself, you know."

"Where are you from?"

"From Ruizele," Roland replied, averting his eyes.

"Quite a long way away."

Roland shrugged. "Half an hour by car, that's all." He opened the hymn book and started thumbing the pages.

Roswita's glance slid past me to him, and I felt chuffed.

"Wait till you see him racing on his bike," I said, for good measure. "He goes so fast he can almost keep up with his father in his Ford Granada."

"My brother's a cyclist too," Roswita said, quite truthfully. He competed in the race at the annual fair, where he would be seen coming up off the saddle for the final spurt, then

73

kissing blondes on the winners' platform and waving bunches of artificial flowers.

Roswita waited for Roland to reply, but he was looking down at his missal and seemed engrossed in a psalm, not realising that his flushed cheeks were making her spine tingle. Even my spine tingled.

The door in the portal down below creaked as it swung open and fell to with a thud: the church was filling up. The altar boys lit the incense. Somewhere behind me air rushed through pallets as the organ inflated its bellows.

A bell tinkled.

Mr Snellaert straightened his back and pulled at the stops.

The organ rumbled in its depths. Valves opened, mouths gaped.

The congregation drew themselves up.

Mr Snellaert nodded, placed his feet on the pedal. Bass tones tickled the lining of my stomach. I was dizzy and shut my eyes.

"Now!" cried Mr Snellaert.

Scales of notes rippled forth. Soaring spirals of tremolos lifted me up even higher than the rood-loft, and from my abdomen gushed the words. "Open the heavenly gates, Oh Lord. Come unto us for Thou art the living Word."

Far beneath me I could hear Roland's pathetically reedy voice. I had left him way behind. My own voice swelled up like a wind-filled sail in perfect trim, no danger of it flapping out of control in my throat today. I soared up straight towards God's glory, but when the last tones died away against the vaulted ceiling and I opened my eyes in blissful contentment, all I saw was Mr Snellaert's stern face.

"Callewijn, if you don't mind," he hissed. "This isn't the opera."

I blushed deep red and sank down on to the bench.

Roland sniggered.

Roswita grinned, chewing her thumb.

*

After mass she sat opposite me in the café and kept glancing at Roland while she fiddled absently with the pack of cards I had brought along.

My cousin had not joined us at our table. He was standing beside my father at the bar, holding his glass of lemonade as if it were beer, rocking on his heels in time to the toasts the men proposed to Roswita's father, a fruit grower who liked to throw his money around.

"Is he staying long?" Roswita asked.

"Dunno. His mother's not too well. It's her nerves."

Roswita said nothing and flicked a lock of hair over her shoulder. Meanwhile, at the bar, things were getting noisy. Red-faced, stabbing the air with his index finger, Roswita's father was the centre of attention. He made some remark which forced the men to think for a second before roaring with laughter. Roland made a show of laughing along with them and sipped his drink.

"Perhaps he could play football with us," Roswita said, with a tremor of maternal concern in her voice. Her father was the chairman of the local club.

"Perhaps. He used to play football, I think." I shrugged and flipped the cards, divided them into piles, shuffled them and laid them out again in a self-invented game without purpose, so as to discourage her from quizzing me further.

In her eyes I was no more than an overgrown toddler, a

not particularly useful guinea pig on whom to practise her flirting skills. On Wednesday afternoons she could be found on a bench in the square by the railway station, holding court in the shade of the plane trees with her ladies-in-waiting casting jealous looks at her precocious figure. All around would be boys practising drop-kicks, dribbles and headers. There was something about her that made me envious, while at the same time I wanted to keep my distance. She could reach you with her invisible tentacles and find out private things. Her presence unsettled the other boys, too, and in her girlfriends, who were otherwise quite ordinary, she inspired a poisonous sort of admiration which made them sullen and prone to lash out with cutting remarks.

I was pleased to see that Roland hardly noticed her when he passed us on his way outside for a pee.

"Tomorrow we'll be going to school together, him and me," I said. "I've got a new bike so I can ride with him."

She didn't respond. Roland had come back. Mumbling about having to ask her father something, she got up from the table and crossed to the men by the bar. Her father stooped willingly when she plucked at his sleeve. She whispered in his ear.

"Is that so?" I heard him say, with a nod in Roland's direction. "At a club or just for fun?"

I couldn't make out Roland's reply, nor whether they were discussing football or cycling, but I noticed him blushing when my father gave him a friendly pat on the shoulder.

"We'll drink to that!" someone exclaimed.

Glasses were raised yet again.

I squeezed the pack of cards with both hands to make it bulge and glanced at the clock over the bar. Half-past one at the latest, my mother had said. It was already a quarter past. We'd be having warmed-up steak again, with reproaches for gravy.

*

It was all set. Toasts had been drunk, his membership of the football club was sealed. Roland would join the team. Practice on Wednesday and Friday evenings. Matches every few weeks on a Saturday.

"And you'll have your choir practice on Thursdays. You'll be busy all week," my father concluded with a satisfied air. My mother was in the kitchen, venting her spleen on the dirty dishes.

"It'd be a good thing for you to take up some sport, too," she called out to me, still angry about her cauliflower boiling to a pulp and her potatoes getting stuck to the bottom of the pan.

She placed the dishes upside down on the draining rack, rubbed some vaseline on her hands and untied her apron, thereby signalling that it was time for the sultry boredom of Sunday afternoon to take over.

Upstairs in my bedroom, with Roland in the next room lying on his bed with a book, I picked up my new satchel and opened it. It was dark brown with long straps to hang over my shoulders so I could carry it on my back. I inspected the stiff leather at close quarters, unzipped the compartments, checked whether my pencil case fitted inside properly and decided on the best places for my sharpener, ruler, rubber, sheets of blotting paper. Once everything was packed away I discovered that the bag was much too light, totally at odds with the weight of the responsibility that I was about to shoulder in

77

the world at large. I added two extra volumes of my father's encyclopaedia and buckled the strap of my satchel, only to discover that it was now so heavy I couldn't lift it off the floor.

"For goodness sake," Roland grumbled, "can't you sit still? You're driving me up the wall with all your fidgeting."

They were the first words he'd spoken to me. Even though I felt a twinge of shame, I lapped them up like honey.

"I've put too much stuff in it," I said.

"In what?"

"My satchel."

He shut his book with a clap. "You don't need to take anything special tomorrow. Just a pen and a pencil. They'll give you all you need at school. They've got their own exercise books, with the name of the school on the front."

Trying to make as little noise as possible, I opened the satchel again and carefully took out one of the volumes, but just as I went to put it on the table it slipped from my fingers and crashed to the floor.

I heard Roland get up and leave the room, slamming the door shut.

It didn't seem a good idea to go after him, however curious I was about what he might be up to.

On his bedside table, next to the imposing alarm clock, lay a book about the Word of God, a gift from an aunt on his mother's side named Vera. It was hard to imagine him wanting to read it, but it lay on top of another book, which was about salmon fishing in Scotland and had lots of photos, and which looked a little more worn than the other one.

The drawer did not contain any vestiges of boyish ruin. No wheels fallen off toy cars, no popguns or plastic geese from a set of farm animals long since dispersed; none of the stuff I kept in the drawer of my own bedside table. I clutched them in my fists like amulets when there was a thunderstorm and I felt I was too old to be scared.

What I found in Roland's drawer was handkerchiefs. All except one, which was stuffed into a corner, lay neatly folded in four little piles. In the compartment underneath there was only an old wristwatch, probably his father's, and a photo of himself smartly dressed for his Holy Communion. That was all I had with which to get a taste of what it was like to be Roland.

I slunk back to my room with an empty feeling, and was relieved when he reappeared a few minutes later to tell me they were having coffee downstairs.

*

That evening he sat beside my father watching a sports programme on television. They clapped their hands on their knees in unison when a favourite player missed the goal by a hair's breadth, and conferred earnestly on the chances of the losing team.

I sat at the table finishing my father's crossword puzzle.

"You can wear your blue shirt tomorrow," my mother said. "You want to look smart for your first day."

Earlier on she had shown me my new sandwich box, which you could squeeze the air out of so as to keep everything fresh. I had nodded admiringly.

Football was followed by a bicycle race. Roland continued to watch with undiminished interest.

My father stood up from his chair. "Join me in a pint, Roland?"

He hesitated for a moment, and then said, "All right. Why not?"

My mother rolled her eyes.

"Ma, please," my father said soothingly. "He's old enough. Besides, drinking takes practice."

"I'll have one too," I ventured.

He didn't answer, just laughed condescendingly.

When he returned with only two bottles from the cellar I folded the newspaper pointedly, kissed my mother goodnight and went upstairs.

I wanted to pack, get ready, and thereby assuage my impatience with rituals, but everything was already in my satchel. I got undressed and lay down on my bed.

The drone from the television downstairs was faintly audible in my room. I turned over on my side and watched the daylight fade.

The drop in temperature made the floorboards shrink again. All the rooms in the house seemed to be filling up with their original occupants. Michel hunting for gin in the dresser. Flora zigzagging towards the bed on her crutches.

"They're in heaven, all of them," my father had said many times.

But what was heaven? Perhaps it was a world that lay above or beneath ours, as transparent as the tissue paper separating the pages of Aunt Odette's photo album.

"There aren't any clocks in heaven," Mr Snellaert had insisted when he was preparing us for our Confirmation. "Just trumpets sounding the Day of Judgement."

Perhaps they were still roaming through the rooms, blind to the new wallpaper, deaf to our conversations. Perhaps they still gathered round the table downstairs in the dead of night or in the middle of what was daytime to us, and did jigsaw puzzles, played cards or darned socks. Now and then, I imagined, Flora would get up, groaning, and drag herself to bed to give birth or to die all over again, after which she would get up again and carry on, according to some logic governed by other-worldly clocks.

The night had grown as dark as their skirts, which my mother had long since thrown away or cut up for use as dust-cloths. I dozed off and didn't know how much later it was when I woke up, from the cold maybe, or from something else. An intriguing sound, there it was again, the rhythmical creaking of bedsprings in Roland's room. It stopped abruptly when I coughed.

I got up and put on my pyjamas. Outside my window, in the dark-blue dusk, hung the full moon. The light shone silver-white on my table, on the lampshade and the handle of my new satchel.

"Roland?" I asked. "Are you awake?"

I heard a deep sigh.

It sounded far too studied for someone who was asleep.

CHAPTER 4

I DREAMED I WAS WEARING a dark suit, jacket and long trousers, shirt and tie, and that my body, although unmistakably mine, was eighteen years old, taut and strong. There were a whole lot of us, a long row filing through a colonnaded passage, or was it a cloistered garden? I was overtaken by someone wearing a brown monk's habit, and in the heat of a June afternoon we lined up on some brick steps between two conifers clipped into conical shapes, just like in the photo propped up against the spines of the encyclopaedias in my father's room downstairs.

My father is holding the school flag at the top of a pyramid of boys with closely cropped heads, under his arm a roll of parchment tied with a narrow scarlet ribbon. Black hair parted down the middle. Two locks falling over his forehead, almost hiding his eyes. He looks grave, concerned almost, as if he already knew that his schooldays were over.

My breast filled with boundless joy, as though something wonderful was afoot, and there we stood, waiting in the shimmering light, perhaps for a photographer to click the shutter.

There was a moment's hush, filled with the twitter of sparrows. The air was electric. Then someone next to me cringed away, and someone else shrieked and covered his face with his hands. From behind me came the sound of breaking glass.

I could hear stones clattering down the tiled roof. In front of me someone collapsed on the ground, as though hit by a bullet. Still more broken glass. The wail of a siren. Someone shouted "Watch out!" I ducked instinctively, but a flying object hit me above my right eye.

It was a while before I realised that I was staring up at the cracks in the ceiling of my room, that I must have been woken by the noise Roland made as he groped sleepily for the alarm clock to silence it.

I stepped out of bed, grabbed a towel and went over to the washbasin.

Roland had opened one baleful eye. For a moment it seemed he was not going to get up, that he would turn over and snuggle down, but then he kicked off the covers and leaped out of bed.

"Move over," he said gruffly. His hair was tousled, as if he'd been swimming across a sea of sheets or burrowing through banks of bed linen until the alarm clock brought release.

We took turns splashing water over our faces, stooping like birds quenching their thirst, craning our necks forward and drawing ourselves up again.

Every time he bent over I stared down at his neck. I noticed several moles, some of them with wiry hairs growing out of them, which were quite unlike the normal hairs that lay flat on his skin. When he clapped his hands to his face and snorted contentedly his shoulder blades stuck out, hard and angular as if he were sprouting wings that cast a shadow over the archipelago of his backbone.

"Get a move on," he grumbled, "it's a quarter past seven already." But it was earlier than ever before. It was the earliest I had ever had to get up.

My eyelids were still heavy with sleep when we went downstairs, where my mother had already put two airtight sandwich boxes side by side on the table.

"Scrambled eggs and bacon," she announced cheerily as she came in from the kitchen with the coffee pot. She proceeded to fill our cups, with remarkably good humour. She was actually humming as she ruffled my hair and leaned across to offer Roland a kiss, which he accepted after a moment's hesitation.

Pink and fluffy in her dressing gown and quilted slippers, my mother sipped her coffee and eyed me with such tenderness that I started chewing more and more slowly, out of sheer apprehension. She wasn't to think I would burst into tears when it was time for us to leave for school.

Meanwhile Roland devoured six slices of bread in quick succession, gulped down his coffee and took a swig of milk. Then he got up, belched, and solemnly said, "Pardon."

"Enjoyed your breakfast?" my mother said, smiling.

He took his plate to the kitchen, despite her protests. "No need to bother, Roland. That's a mother's work."

Turning to me, she laid her hand on my cheek. "Fancy having to let you go already…"

I pulled away. "My shoes," I said.

I had put on my ankle boots, which came close to being as clumpy as the black leather clogs that Roland wore. Shoes with thick soles, which made me at least two centimetres taller, but they had complicated laces. They reached out in meandering labyrinthine coils and laid themselves in nasty knots when I tried to deal with them unaided.

"You should really start tying your own laces, you know," my mother said, with a rueful sigh. She kneeled down at my feet.

"You will take care, won't you?" she said with a catch in her throat. "Just you stick close to Roland, mind."

I was glad I couldn't see her fighting back her tears.

*

Roland took the lead as we rode over the dyke, both with our satchels on our backs. It was a pale morning, neither sunny nor cloudy. Swathes of mist drifted over the water and further on, where the canal curved and widened out, the houses and trees were veiled in grey. We cycled alongside the warehouses with fork-lift trucks riding in and out, past the flour mill where strange funnels suspended from cranes sucked up the cargo of ships moored alongside in a cloud of fine yellow dust. On some days I would catch sight of my father at work there. He'd look up if I rang my bell, but today he was nowhere to be seen.

All the way up to the railway crossing the world was familiar to me. I had explored the sandy lanes, knew where everyone lived and which guard dogs I had to beware of, and could locate the bomb craters that had turned into ponds alive with the whirr of dragonflies making rainbows with their wings. The stretch of open countryside came to an end in a thickly canopied wood.

There, under the trees, it smelled of damp earth, of fermentation and mould. The first toadstools were shooting up in the verges. Peering through the gaps in the rhododendron bushes, I could make out the castle at the end of the drive. That was as far as I had ever ventured on my bicycle, before racing back the way I came for fear of getting lost in the web of lanes.

The park was deserted. Peacocks strutted about on the lawn, dragging their tails behind them. Magpies chattered in the depths of the wood. Pigeons circled around the roofs of the farmhouses at the far end.

"Can you keep up?" Roland panted.

"No problem," I cried, although my calves were aching and the saddle was beginning to hurt my thighs.

The trees thinned out. Through the brushwood a pool sparkled, with little islands rising like ruined fortresses above the mist and fringes of reed. We came upon an open space. There were fields, some of which had been parcelled into plots where villas were under construction. Still further on the road made a sharp turn, and we were riding under the trees again, but uphill now. Roland stood up on the pedals. I broke out in a sweat.

At the top we found ourselves in a busy settlement of houses, with bicycles pouring on to the road from all sides.

"Hey Roland, have you moved house or something?" someone called in passing.

"Hi," Roland called back, without bothering to look who it was.

I kept my eyes fixed ahead, anxious not to get tangled with the other bikes on the road. By the time we reached the high street the stream of cyclists had swollen to a swarm, a plague of locusts surging past the houses, crossing the market square with the bandstand and sliding into a narrow side street.

A few hundred metres on, surrounded by wasteland where stretches of newly constructed roads stopped abruptly as though the houses they led to had yet to rise from the ground, stood our school.

I had imagined crenellations, ramparts and walls overgrown with ivy or woodbine; that I would be entering a world of study and respectful silence, with deeply shaded galleries and turrets like minarets, and a drawbridge; but what I saw was more like a stack of shoeboxes, austere and white, with cold steel window frames. One of the boxes had a low gateway, into which plunged the horde of bicycles.

I had trouble keeping up with Roland. In the end I lost sight of him and simply followed the others into a gloomy space with concrete pillars and bicycle racks.

Boys got down from their saddles, exchanging noisy greetings. I threaded my way through them cautiously, until my ear was pulled hard. A man with a face like a lump of dough barked at me that cycling was not allowed past the gateway. "Got that?"

I parked my bike in one of the racks, feeling weak at the knees. I spotted Roland in the mêlée spilling out over the bleak, paved courtyard, but when I went up to him he didn't seem keen to have me around.

"You're supposed to stay on that side," he drawled, pointing to a white line crossing the school yard from end to end, dividing it exactly in two.

On the far side gangly youths bounced basketballs on the pavement. The near side, reserved for juniors, was occupied by lads lugging outsized satchels, circling each other warily, breaking ranks again and picking at their pimples.

I saw Roland go up to a group of boys who greeted him warmly. Punches were exchanged, playful blows were dodged. Someone held him fast, made him bend over and swiped off his cap.

I retraced my steps. The chap with the doughy face was

87

walking back and forth along the white line like a border guard, and kept glancing in my direction.

Of all the things I had seen in my father's photographs, only the monastery with its frail cupolas and pretty bay windows was still standing. Wedged in among a couple of the shoeboxes, the old building seemed to tremble while it was being slowly squashed.

There were tufts of grass growing on the brick steps where my father had once raised the school flag, and the conifers must have been chopped down ages ago. In the middle of a small, fussy flower bed stood a weather-beaten Christ spreading his arms, one of which had been amputated at the elbow, either due to a mishap or to mischief.

There was no horizon anywhere. No way out. Not even when I looked up. The sky was a rectangular hole with a lid of clouds.

This was St Joseph's Institute for Hopeless Education, where it snowed chalk-dust, the sterile pollen of learning, day in day out. Where all the classrooms were equipped with centrally driven clocks swotting the minutes away like so many flies. Where tired kaffir lilies in pots on the window sills struggled to produce the bloom that might well be their last.

I picked my way cautiously across the school yard, avoiding throngs of arguing boys, and positioned myself against the wall at the far end. A stale, sour-sweet smell from the stairs leading up to the classrooms wafted towards me. It was as though everything had been treated with a secret substance, not for the purpose of banishing the fluffy detritus from hundreds of jumpers, the smell of farts, belches, badly brushed teeth, the stench of countless armpits, but on the contrary to preserve them and mix them all up in a potent, all-enveloping atmosphere: that of school. More vividly than any punish-ment it was the institutional fug that brought home to me that school had reduced me to a cipher, one of the herd. Part sheep ready for slaughter, part insect; a creature with spindly, puny bones, rising saps and a nervous system like an over-twigged fruit tree in dire need of pruning.

*

A bell shrilled out. The older boys straggled into the building for class. The chap with the dough-face called out, "New boys assemble in front of the monastery."

Someone had thought to place a microphone on the ter-race. Two of the bay windows were wide open and had loudspeakers on the sills.

I hung around at the back of the group. A boy with long fair hair said, "Hello. I'm Willem," and extended his hand.

"I'm Anton," I said, somewhat taken aback by his friendliness.

"Do you live in Ruizele?"

I shook my head. "No, in Stuyvenberghe. It's not far from here."

"I live in the woods near here," he said. "My father's an architect," he added, as if the two were connected.

He spoke in a soft, well-mannered kind of way, which I found just as pleasing as his hair. But the others thought he sounded funny: they glanced at him and sniggered.

He was not one of us. The speech patterns underlying his language were different. He did not have the musty, cavernous tone that distinguished the regional accent, instead he spoke in a leisurely, mellifluous sing-song.

"So what does your Pa do?" he asked.

"We used to farm," I said.

He did not pursue the subject.

The door of the monastery opened and a short, doll-like figure emerged. He stepped daintily to the microphone, adjusted his brown Homburg hat, slipped his hand into the pocket of his fluttering nylon raincoat and drew out a pair of gold-rimmed spectacles. He put them on with a flourish of the fingers.

"That's Father Deceuster," Willem said. "He's the principal. A do-gooder."

The priest unfolded a sheet of paper with delicate movements. A pause ensued, during which he eyed us sharply. When he finally pronounced the words "Good morning young men", we all started at the volume of his voice.

His booming salutation was instantly met with a tinny screech from the loudspeakers blaring out over the brick paving.

The priest took his spectacles off and hissed, "François, François!"

The man with the dough-face tiptoed to the front, made a reassuring gesture and ran inside. The screeching stopped.

Recovering himself, the priest readjusted his glasses and said, "You have just made the acquaintance of Mr Bouillie! Devoted study supervisor and a pillar of this institution. A round of applause for Mr Bouillie!"

A couple of boys started clapping dutifully. Willem kept his hands in his pockets.

The priest considered this to be a blessed day, for it was the first day not only of term but also of the school year, which meant that we were embarking on a great adventure.

"He says the same thing every year," Willem murmured. "He'll be telling us about the new sports hall next."

"This school is ready and waiting for you," the priest said, beaming. "With all the proper modern facilities, and we are proud—as I'm sure you'll agree, Mr Bouillie—to announce that the new sports hall can finally, yes finally, be put to use. From now on we play basketball indoors and we swim in our own private pool!"

"It took him fifty seafood banquets to raise the funds," Willem said. "My father couldn't stand it any more. After the third one he wrote a cheque. That stopped them."

"… and then our entirely renovated typing classroom," the priest continued, "for which Mr Villeyn has quite rightly been campaigning for years."

"Villeyn, rhymes with villain," Willem murmured.

I wondered how he knew all these things. "Have you got an older brother here by any chance?"

He avoided my eye. "I've been put back a year. Tried too hard."

Father Deceuster looked ecstatic, as if he were about to levitate. He held forth about a schoolboy's duty to be a good Christian and drifted into a muddled discourse on happiness, which in his view was to be found in little things. Screwing up his notes, he wished us a good term and good progress on our road to a strong and healthy adolescence.

There was a feeble round of applause.

Mr Bouillie took a brisker line. He took the mike from the priest and barked, "I am going to call out your names followed by an A, a B or a C. After roll-call I shall give you a signal for you to go to the teacher holding your designated letter."

He pointed to the far end of the yard, where three teachers were standing on the step in front of a wooden gate, each holding up a sign.

I was given a B.

So was Willem.

"We'll be together, then," I said.

We crossed the yard and went to our respective teachers.

"It's Vaneenooghe," Willem said, "which isn't too bad. He teaches religious education."

"I want you to file in an orderly fashion and I don't want to hear another word," Mr Vaneenooghe said.

He paused. "Not another word," he repeated.

When everyone was quiet he snapped his fingers.

The row started moving.

Willem nudged me.

Mr Vaneenooghe pushed against the gate, which swung wide open as if it were the mouth of hell.

CHAPTER 5

A FLIGHT OF BLUESTONE STEPS took us to the upper level, where neon strip lights flickered. We filed down a narrow passage with wood panelling along one wall. The other wall had high windows through which you could see grey sky, lamp-posts, and a cable swaying in the breeze.

Mr Vaneenooghe held open the door of our cage. He ushered us in with a gallant bow. "Do come in, gentlemen," he said.

We were surrounded by stark green walls, the only relief being a crucifix hanging slightly askew over the blackboard and a faded poster showing a lad chewing a straw. The caption underneath read, "Hope is the Fountain of Youth."

The wood of the desks was far too hard to carve your name in the surface, the gleaming varnish was indestructible. I picked a desk in the middle, somewhat nearer to the door than to the blackboard.

"Mind if I sit next to you?" Willem asked.

I said I didn't mind.

We both looked on with interest as a young lad in front of us unzipped his school bag lovingly and took out a tartan pencil case, a sharpener in the shape of a cow, a wooden ruler, a pair of compasses, a protractor, a bicoloured rubber, a marker pen and two tubes of glue. He crossed his arms in eager readiness, and seemed somewhat taken aback when Mr Vaneenooghe instructed us to raise the lids of our desks.

"You'll find all the exercise books you need inside," he said.

Each exercise book had a photograph of a school on the cover—all of them different but all run by the same religious order. The same shoeboxes everywhere, the same paved school yard. No doubt they all had their own Mr Bouillies to patrol their borders.

Disheartened, I rested the lid against my forehead.

"Anything wrong?" Willem asked.

I shook my head.

"You can take them home with you after school today," Mr Vaneenooghe continued, "so you can put your names and numbers on the covers." There were dotted lines to indicate where. Everything had been thought out beforehand, nothing would be left to chance.

Back at my old school Mr Snellaert would be herding a new flock into his classroom, where the walls were covered in photographs and postcards. Sums would become palpable as if by magic, as real as the click of the beads on the old-fashioned abacus he still used. On the walls he would unroll maps as big as Gobelin tapestries, he would usher his pupils into the great halls of history and unfold Belgium as if it were an imaginary kingdom encompassing regions such as Lorraine, with its sombre resonance of Teutonic ruins. Harnessed in his grey suit of armour he was ever on the alert for the slightest sign of a scaly claw, a forked tongue, so that he might sally forth and save us from the demon of boredom.

Mr Vaneenooghe, on the other hand, seemed to have stepped straight out of a cut-price clothing store. His suit looked as though it was still on the hanger as he moved stiffly about the classroom. His enthusiasm, however, was clearly moth-eaten.

Making a pretence of geniality, he perched on the corner of his desk and waited patiently until we had all stored away our exercise books. Then he got up and crossed to the blackboard. He let out an exaggerated sigh as he picked a piece of chalk from the ridge and wrote in capital letters GOD IS OUR BEST FRIEND. He turned round to face us and rubbed his hands while a plaster smile peeled from his lips.

*

During midday break I saw Roland again. He was sitting at the far end of the refectory with five of his mates, close to the podium where Father Deceuster had appeared a moment before to make the sign of the cross and wish us "a pleasant meal", whereupon the clatter of spoons in soup bowls took over and I wrenched the lid off my sandwich box.

Willem had gone home. I was surrounded by boys I had no inclination to get to know any better. They were chattering away, undaunted by Mr Bouillie, who was on the prowl among the tables for irregularities of behaviour.

Here too, seniors and juniors were kept apart. The hall was divided down the middle by a step. From the lower section the deep voices of the older boys floated up to me, and I wondered whether I would ever thrive in these surroundings like they did, quite uninhibited by the sense that it was all a farce.

At half-past one we went outside. Basketballs bounced out of the shed into the school yard. A boy asked me if I wanted to join in, but I declined the offer. I wanted to be invisible, to blend into the brick and concrete background like a chameleon, and later on, when the bell rang to signal that it was time to go home, to take on the colour of grass and trees again. But effacement was impossible. No matter how hard I tried to avoid being noticed, I kept feeling Mr Bouillie's eyes boring into my shoulders.

Still, there were certain places that seemed to elude his omnipresence. Blind corners at the back of the bike shed, by the gymnasium wall, where hastily stubbed-out ciggies, sweet wrappers and general litter suggested clandestine delights, quick, urgent and sweet.

On the far side of the yard, where it adjoined the monastery, Roland and his mates huddled together by an overgrown laurel bush. Mr Bouillie was at the opposite end, working his beat with the assurance that is the preserve of the truly mighty. His movements were predictable, like the passage of a comet or a shower of meteors, and for the moment he was well out of range.

A frivolous curl of smoke rose from the leafy bush. A few boys on the lookout gestured a warning, taking care not to attract too much attention. By the time Mr Bouillie came round again, they had dispersed into pairs or threesomes, conversing casually as if nothing had happened.

I hoped Willem would be back soon, but yet another bell rang out, this time for us to return to the refectory. When we had all taken our places at the tables, which had been cleared in the meantime, Mr Bouillie snapped his fingers to signal the start of an hour of silent study.

Once I had written my name down on the covers of my exercise books I couldn't think of anything else to do. The smell of soup still lingered in the air over the tables, and the only sounds intruding on the silence were Mr Bouillie's steady footfalls and the odd slap of a ruler being brought down too brusquely.

The other boys at my table were busy doing sums. I took as long as I could to write my name down, after which I opened my R.E. exercise book and reread what Mr Vaneenooghe had made us write down about God, Whose hand was ever on our shoulders, either in encouragement or in fatherly reproof.

We had been told to draw a circle. "If you take the dot in the middle to be God," Mr Vaneenooghe had said, "you can add another dot to indicate your own position."

I would have preferred to put myself somewhere outside the circle, but had the feeling that this wouldn't be considered right.

"Aha, a marginal position yet again," Mr Vaneenooghe had said with a glance at my drawing, while his beard crinkled around a threadbare smile.

I was interrupted in my musings by the clatter of a pen falling on the floor and the scrape of a chair. I turned round and saw Mr Bouillie grabbing one of the new boys by the nape of the neck and holding him out in front of him like a rag.

"No fidgeting during study hour!" he scolded, pushing the boy up the steps to the podium, where he had to stand with his back to the rest of us and "think things over".

Stifled sobs could be heard in the refectory. Mr Bouillie adjusted the cuffs of his jacket and went about his business.

I sat there wishing I could erect a sort of electric fence all around me, the way they did in the science-fiction comics I was addicted to. An invisible, impenetrable dome, inside which I could seal myself off from the surrounding moonscape and at the same time prevent the hatred that was oozing from all my pores from being noticed by everyone. I clenched my teeth and put little pencil marks in the margins of my exercise book.

The afternoon dragged on. Lessons started again at half-past two. The clouds lifted briefly, and the most excruciating boredom I had ever experienced came pouring in through the tall windows.

A man wearing a wide tie and pebble glasses opened his briefcase. He instructed me to say what my name was in French: "Je m'appelle Antoine." "Et vous?" he inquired, turning to Willem. "Mon nom est Guillaume," he replied. He was obliged to add "J'ai aussi une petite soeur. Elle s'appelle Kathérine." He glanced at me sheepishly.

The wide tie was followed by a skinny fellow wearing a foul-smelling jumper. He unrolled a miserable little map against the blackboard showing Belgium's major concentrations of industry, all the sectors of which he proceeded to enumerate in the humdrum drone of a fly buzzing aimlessly around a lamp.

Willem sprawled at his desk. "I could just do with a good kip."

He cracked his knuckles.

"De Vries, sit up straight. No slouching or slacking in my class," came the voice from the blackboard.

Willem drew himself up slowly, drummed his fingers on the top of his desk and puffed out his cheeks.

"Moron," I heard him whisper.

*

The four o'clock bell unleashed anarchy. Mr Bouillie stood in the flurry of departing bicycles, flailing his arms as if he were trying to net a school of herrings and hated to see any escape.

Roland was cycling way ahead of me and Willem. He was in a team with his mates, talking and shouting, but they fell silent at a stroke when they spotted a bunch of fluttery schoolgirls in blue uniforms starting off home on their bikes.

The girls stopped en masse by the bandstand on the square, dismounted and tied their jerseys around their hips to shorten their skirts. They were like wading birds on the shore of a lake, chattering away, darting looks at the boys dawdling by the cafés on the edge of the square, bouncing the frames of their bikes against their thighs as they talked.

"Do you want to hang about for a bit?" Willem asked, hunched nonchalantly over his handlebars.

"My father said I should stick with my cousin over there," I said.

Roland did not seem to be in the slightest hurry. He had tied his jacket on his luggage carrier and had rolled up his shirt-sleeves, and was now deep in discussion with some other boys.

The atmosphere was tense. Surreptitious looks flashed to and fro. Racy comments ricocheted off the pavement. The girls would be flapping their wings and taking off next.

"You'll be taking the road through the wood, won't you?" Willem said. "We can wait for him there."

We crossed the market square on our way out of Ruizele and cycled uphill, not stopping until we reached the point where the road plunged in among the trees.

Willem pulled back his long hair into a ponytail, which he secured with an elastic band.

"It's not allowed at school," he said.

Leaning on his handlebars with his arms crossed, he gazed out over the roofs, the hospital grounds and the church tower with gold lettering over the belfry: *Destructa 1914—Resurrecta 1920,* it said.

"Are you always so serious?" he asked.

"Dunno…" I said haltingly. I had never thought about myself in those terms, really. Maybe that's what I was: serious.

I knew I had been much jollier in the past, when there was a heap of parcels under the Christmas tree or when it was my birthday. But none of the presents I'd had for my first Communion a couple of months ago had given me the same kind of thrill.

Even my elation at Uncle Roger's gift of a wristwatch had been short-lived, for it was too blatant a reminder of the rules and duties that would govern me from now on. You had to see to it that it didn't run ahead of the proper time or slow down and even stop altogether. The face had a little window showing the date, which changed all by itself at midnight exactly. I knew this because I'd stayed awake on purpose. The next morning my thumb was sore from the grooves on the winder.

Time was something I wanted to get away from. I had the feeling that my new school was nothing but a front for a factory or military laboratory, where time was a weird, newly discovered serum that was injected directly into our veins in order to test how much of it we could take without falling asleep or becoming unruly. Even the soup which we were served daily—and which, so I discovered later, got thinner and thinner from Monday to Friday until it was little more than water with flecks of green—had time floating in it.

I heard Willem snigger.

"Dreamer," he said.

I wasn't dreaming. There was too much too look at, too much to see. My eyes were funnels into which the world kept pouring images. The real homework I had to do each evening was to sort all these impressions, classify them, put them in little boxes, fit them together like a jigsaw puzzle so they wouldn't hang around in the night and get tangled in my sheets.

Why was Roland the way he was? He was pedalling up the slope towards us, chattering to his mates. Why did everything about him seem to fit? He talked in the same way as he pedalled his bike: in a no-nonsense, blunt kind of way. His thoughts resembled massive cupboards in his head. They remained shut until the ground tilted suddenly and the contents tumbled out like saucepans clattering to the floor. Compared to him I was a servant girl: furtively opening drawers, taking dresses from wardrobes and holding them against my front in the mirror, making sure to put the clothes back without creasing them.

He and his mates ignored us as they rode past.

Willem swung his bike round. We freewheeled down the slope under the trees. The past couple of hours slithered away like water off a duck's back.

That very morning I had cycled past his house without knowing that he lived there. It was on the corner between two avenues. The gaps in the rhododendrons showed glimpses of a big garden. I noted a slide, and a gaily coloured sculpture on the lawn: a roly-poly woman with flowers painted all over her. The house loomed in the shadows. It was rather peculiar, dark and greenish with streaks of damp on the concrete exterior. The curving walls with large windows seemed to have been designed to spare as many trees as possible.

"Thank goodness that's it for today," said Willem. He swerved into the front garden and made for a mass of honeysuckle and ivy with a carport underneath and a glass door.

"I'll wait for you here," he said. "See you tomorrow."

"See you."

I sped away, pedalling hard to catch up with Roland.

CHAPTER 6

T HE DAYS SHORTENED APACE. The dusk, which was already gathering when Roland and I went home after school, deepened each day. At home, the flames in the stove leaped higher and higher behind the sooty window, while the kettle sang that it was winter. We all moved closer together as the weather got colder.

Those were the weeks when the sky switched direction. Orion rose to its zenith, there was turbulence in the air, and gusts of wind buffeted the walls and hooked their fingers behind the shutters, making the woodwork rattle on its hinges.

Autumn was never my favourite season. From the end of August on I felt as if the summer were unwinding, like knitting being unravelled to save the wool, which would be rolled up into balls and stored away out of reach. As it was, the autumn showers and early storms seemed to be in tune with my soul, similarly in a state of flux.

One evening my mother came into the bathroom just as I was towelling myself dry. "Pardon," she said, and left quickly. Later on I heard her on the phone to one of her sisters, saying that I was getting to be a big lad and that I was an early starter, seeing as I was only just twelve.

"Oh well," she said. "Our Alois was rather forward, too,

and so were you: your periods started when you were eleven, didn't they?"

"Early birds, eh," I heard her say with a chuckle before replacing the receiver.

When I saw myself in the mirror I looked pretty much as usual from the waist up, except maybe for some blotches on my forehead. But if I lowered my gaze and contemplated the dark curly hair of my crotch, a dense thicket surrounding that thing between my legs, I felt as if a macabre joke were being played on me: I was turning into an animal.

I wondered whether I was the only one to be plagued thus, whether anybody else was obliged to shift around in their seat like me, when my veins started throbbing for no apparent reason, when the lining of my stomach tingled and the thing in my underpants insisted on swelling up. However tightly I clenched my thighs, I couldn't stop it from poking out from under my waistband and stretching the elastic in a way that made me shudder.

When this happened in class I sat very still for a time, glancing round to see if anyone had noticed, especially Willem, who never seemed to be bothered by these things.

Mr Vaneenooghe had mentioned "certain changes", and had announced a special slide-show entitled "Growth and Tenderness", but it didn't amount to anything more exciting than boys and girls holding hands as they strolled down meadows and country lanes.

The images were accompanied by a cassette tape with trumpets and a soppy voice-over. For the rest, God's top priority appeared to be personal hygiene. Mr Vaneenooghe had pronounced the words as if he had a hair stuck between his teeth.

During the school medical examination the doctor had pulled down my underpants, told me to blow on my hand, and then kneaded me with cold fingers. He ticked a box on the form, muttering, "That looks fine."

I had asked Willem if the doctor had said the same about him. But Willem had frowned, and I didn't dare pursue it any further.

The whole afternoon had been awful. First a nurse made me open my mouth wide so she could tap an instrument against each of my teeth in turn. Then she made me bend over, whereupon she drew my buttocks apart with her thumb and index finger. Then she put earphones on my head and went half-crazy when I had trouble telling left from right.

She heaved a sigh and pushed me into a lavatory. There was a hatch in one of the walls with a glass measuring cup, which I took in my hands doubtfully. It was only after several minutes, when she knocked on the door asking, "Still not done?" that the penny dropped.

*

If only I could leave it all behind, find some groove in a tree trunk where I could spin a silk cocoon around myself and go to sleep for as long as it took to transform into a different state. But at night, in the soothing darkness, the ache in my joints often kept me awake. In heavy weather the storms raging outside seemed to be coming directly from within me. There were nights when I woke up drenched, with the thing refusing point-blank to lie down. I would try to find some relief in the familiar sounds of Roland asleep, unless he was awake too, in which case I could tell by his hushed breathing that he was waiting for me to doze off.

Three days a week he came home with wet hair, making the air redolent with the fresh mud he scraped off his football boots as he sat on the doorstep. The towels he pulled out of his sports bag were so suffused with his odour, the excruciating tang of his sweat, that an invisible twin of his seemed to emerge when he draped them over the footboard of his bed.

The way he shovelled down his food, swigged his drink and broke wind without any shame at all was something I secretly envied, just as I envied the subtle witchcraft with which Roswita was able to shatter his confidence at a stroke.

Up in the rood-loft she had unceremoniously ousted me from my seat a few weeks after his arrival, and had inserted herself with matriarchal aplomb between him and me. The things she whispered to him in the intervals between songs clearly made him uneasy.

He stuck his hands between his knees and awkwardly rubbed his palms together. Roswita's girlfriends were watching him narrowly, nudging each other. They appeared to be in the know regarding her sophisticated strategies and made mental notes of the times he blushed, as if they were goals she had scored.

*

They went to nearly every match. Roswita's father offered everyone drinks in the canteen, in the hope of making mayor one day. Roswita herself was usually to be found with her entourage under the corrugated iron roof by the changing rooms. She cheered when goals were scored, booed when they were missed, and stayed until the umpire blew his whistle and the teams left the pitch.

"You're a fine runner, Roland," she would shout. "My father says so too."

That was enough to make him blush to the roots of his hair and keep his head down as he made for the changing room.

Inside was full of hot steam. Now and then, when the door opened a crack, I glimpsed him standing under the shower with his eyes closed, surrounded by a blur of bodies braying to each other in a show of unconcern over their nakedness.

Sometimes he would bray like that at home, too, after he'd washed and begun to put his clothes on. He always fussed with his underpants, tucking his buttocks in carefully, and then stretching out the waistband with his thumbs to inspect his crotch.

I took malicious pleasure in observing him. Knowing that he was at his most vulnerable, I dipped my words thoughtfully in poison and took very careful aim before letting fly.

"Everything all right then, Roland? Hasn't shrunk has it?"

"Don't stare. Mind your own business, you little creep."

"I thought you liked me looking at you."

Usually he would shut up after that and continue to get dressed.

*

When I was around Willem I was just as likely to be tongue-tied as Roland was when Roswita put her feelers out towards him. Willem was a lot less talkative than the others. He wasn't as withdrawn as I was, but I never saw him being mobbed by friends the way Roland constantly was.

Usually I was the only company he had. We crossed and re-crossed the school yard side by side, and while we surveyed the bleak surroundings, intent on deleting whatever we found offensive, we ourselves were constantly being watched by Mr Bouillie. In his routinely disdainful air there was a trace of suspicion. He couldn't place us. We weren't sissies, nor were we rebels. We got reasonably good marks, in class we made sure we were not overeager while being sufficiently attentive, but when we raised our hackles we did it together. As a two-some we were unassailable. If we got the chance we preferred hanging around in remote corners, around the bike shed or in the shaded colonnade, where scraps of paper blew around in little whirlwinds. This was frowned on by Mr Bouillie.

"Callewijn," he had said one day, after midday break. "You seem to get on remarkably well with De Vries."

"Yes, sir."

"What about the other boys? The two of you seem to stick together all the time."

"Yes, sir."

"You need to integrate with the rest, you know. Do you good…"

I didn't know what "integrate" meant.

"He's being easy on us," Willem told me. "Because of my Pa. The fund-raising."

If I kept my eyes peeled, if I made a convincing show of obeying the rules and overcame my boredom, it had to be possible to fathom the hidden agenda of school. That way I could endure the humiliations with my head held high and come out at the end more or less unscathed.

The first swimming session proved to be good practice. On the day itself I was already nervous when I left home in the morning. In the cubicle Willem and I shared, I made myself as small as possible. We both tried to avoid bumping into each other, and if we did we mumbled a quick "sorry". I put off stripping to the buff as long as I could.

His body made me feel inadequate. Nature had cast him from a perfect mould, unlike me. I looked as if I was made up of odds and ends. One of my nipples was lower than the other, and also stuck out more. The hollow in my chest was too deep for my liking. I kept getting red bumps on my buttocks, which made them look like unripe berries with lots of hair in between.

The swimming trunks that my mother had undoubtedly ferreted out of some cut-price treasure trove, a shapeless garment with brown stripes and orange dots, did not make me feel any better. They contrasted shrilly with Willem's tasteful navy-blue trunks, which he had put on whistling. Besides, he had shed his clothes without the least sign of embarrassment.

He had blond hair. All his hair was blond. Beneath his navel, the base of his belly was fringed with pleasing flaxen curls, and the secret part down in the furrow between his thighs had no doubt been pronounced very fine indeed by the school doctor.

He moved with a self-assurance that seemed to have more to do with the harmonious proportions of his body than with his state of mind, and it made me long for something I couldn't quite grasp. The promise of boundless blessing, the sense of dissolving in time, of being able to open out like a shell and escape from my own skinny self.

His limbs, like Roland's, seemed a perfect fit. His body expressed him quite satisfactorily, it rarely interrupted him. He didn't have arms that felt like too-long sleeves that got in the way. He kept his arms crossed on his desk or let them hang down in a very relaxed sort of way when he leaned back in his chair, whereas I just wished that mine were at least five centimetres shorter. Mine kept letting me down, they were the source of my clumsiness.

He tapped me on the nose.

"You're miles away. Come on."

Mr Bruane, the P.E. teacher, who'd had the septum removed from his nose because it had been an impediment to his boxing career, had already clapped his hands, at which the doors of the cubicles had all swung open.

I waited for the last pair of bare feet to patter past on the wet tiles before stepping out of my cubicle.

We had to line up on the edge of the pool. Mr Bruane ordered us to jump into the water one by one and to swim two lengths.

I managed to turn a deaf ear to the surreptitious sniggering and thought I would make it to the end without incurring too much abuse, until Mr Bruane told me to get up on the diving board and make a dive exactly as he had personally demonstrated moments before.

There I stood, in all my misery, having to endure the jeers of my classmates with their smart trunks and even tans from Marseilles or St Tropez. Nor did the amusement in the swimming instructor's eyes escape me.

"Cal-le-wijn! Cal-le-wijn!" they shouted.

I steeled myself, took a deep breath and shut my eyes.

The arc I described in the air can't have been very elegant. The water hit me like a fist in the stomach, and for an instant I heard a great roar.

Then it was quiet. Blue light, a froth of bubbles. Panic. My own flailing arms and legs.

When I came up for air the others had gone, all except Willem.

He stretched his arms along the little gutter just above the surface of the pool and eyed me uneasily while I hid my tears with both my hands.

"Come on out. Time to go."

I shook my head vigorously. "Can't…"

He waited.

"Callewijn! Can't get enough of the water all of sudden, eh?" Mr Bruane called. There was a fresh roar from the cubicles.

"Come on."

"Leave me alone."

"You'll get into trouble."

I gave him a long hard look.

He didn't get it at first. Then he rolled his eyes, let go of the edge and disappeared under water.

It was a while before he resurfaced, with my trunks. He handed them over to me with a straight face.

"Don't ever let on," he said later on in the changing cubicle. "They can scent it. They're like wolves. They always pick on the runt of the litter."

I dried my tears, nodded.

"They're good at that."

He swore to himself, slipped his jacket on and buttoned up his sports bag.

He was already near to the exit. I hesitated before calling him back.

He swung round.

"What?"

My cheeks burned.

"Could you help me do up my laces?"

CHAPTER 7

T HAT AUTUMN, as I remember it, was bathed in the diffuse light of an overcast sky and the stillness of October, when the dyke was permanently shrouded in mist and it drizzled for days on end.

It was the autumn when I became suddenly and acutely aware that my father's hair was turning grey, especially around his ears. It hit me one evening during supper. He had been working late, and while he ate he complained bitterly about the situation at the mill, where things were looking bad.

"It's just getting crazier every year," he confided in me.

With each mouthful his anger ebbed away. I could see him sinking back into his usual self-absorption. Now and then a muttered imprecation bubbled up from his chest, then it was all over. He laid the newspaper on the table next to his plate, and started to read.

He's getting old, I thought, and I was shocked. His father, whom I had never met, had turned white by the age of thirty. There were photographs to prove it. But thirty was old. In those days people were either little, big, or old. My father had always been big. Being big meant casting a big shadow, like the spread of leafy branches. I had nestled in his arms as if they were the limbs of a tree.

Now I was getting big myself. Even my mother said so. And he said so too, on days when I skulked around the house, pestering Roland, flinging myself dramatically on my bed, slamming doors, leaving my shoes lying in the middle of the room instead of putting them on the rack, at which he would jump up from his chair and demand in a puzzled tone of voice, "Anton, boy, whatever's the matter?"

"I don't know," I would yell, bounding up the stairs. "Everything."

When the storm had subsided he came up to my room and sat on the edge of my bed. After a long silence he said, "You're getting to be a big boy."

He needed reading glasses to do his crossword. They magnified his eyes, and the helpless astonishment with which they seemed to view the world filled me with a deepening sense of weariness. My father, old. The thought repelled me. So did his shuffling footsteps on the bathroom tiles. And so did his hand on my shoulders when he came in while I was doing my homework and said, "Mourning song. Five letters. Latin."

"*Nenia*, Pa."

He kept forgetting. He couldn't find the words he was looking for. When Roswita's father turned up in the café on Sunday, he hunched his shoulders. When he spoke I could hear him rattling coins and keys in his trouser pockets to help him think.

I registered these things. I was growing up. He was growing down in my eyes. I was growing right up over the roof and the stables. My thoughts branched out. In the old days when things were always out of reach and I longed to be as tall as the cupboards, being grown-up had struck me as a tranquil state in which to be. But it wasn't easy getting there. It was Willem's fault. I felt myself clambering up inside his tall body and looking out at the world through his eyes.

One Wednesday afternoon I fetched up at his house. Roland had gone to visit his father. It was pouring with rain. After fifty metres our coats were soaked through.

"You'd better shelter in our house until there's a break," he said and I followed him on my bike into the garage.

We left our shoes on the mat. He opened a door for me and led me across a grey-green carpet into a long corridor, which was entirely made of glass on one side. I followed him up the stairs to his bedroom. He grabbed some towels from a cupboard and threw one in my direction.

We rubbed ourselves dry, hung our trousers over the backs of chairs and sat down at his desk by the window, looking out on the dripping trees. We rolled a marble back and forth over his desktop for a while. He showed me his books. Quite a lot of them were about natural history, which I wasn't too keen on. He played me his records. A din, to my ears.

He straightened his bedcover and lay down on top, folded his arms behind his head, got up again and handed me a pair of his trousers to put on. He folded the bottoms up over my ankles so I wouldn't trip.

Then came that strange moment, when he'd gone to the lavatory and his mother came up the stairs with a laundry basket and paused on the landing, said hello, asked who I was and looked me up and down for a very long time.

I lowered my eyes, studied the bookcase and stared at my fingers.

When I raised my eyes again she was halfway down the corridor. As she turned into another room I heard her say,

"Katrien, if you aren't practising, you'd better close the lid. Or the keys will just gather dust." Someone started banging on a piano.

"Is your friend staying for supper?" she asked when we came downstairs.

"You staying for lunch?" Willem echoed, as if I hadn't understood what she'd said.

"Dunno… I expect they'll be wondering where I've got to, back home."

"Well, we can give them a bell," she said. "What's your number?"

She addressed my mother with the words, "Good afternoon, this is Willem's mother. We've saved someone from drowning here."

I knew my mother wouldn't have a clue what she meant. I could hear her halting voice from where I was standing, offering apologies, hoping that I was not causing any trouble.

"He's drenched to the skin, you know. His clothes are drying upstairs."

I had to be home by five o'clock.

*

Willem's house breathed. It soaked up daylight through all its vast windows. It sprawled on to the lawn and looked at the trees. Inside, there were long sofas upholstered in leather and low wall cabinets with large paintings hanging above them, oblongs of evenly coloured mist. Out in the garden the roly-poly statue danced in the rain.

His father came down another staircase from his office. He shook hands with me. The table was laid for five.

"Enjoy your meal, children," he said, spreading his linen napkin on his lap.

They spoke in a posh accent, with the kind of ease that would have had my father fumbling desperately in his pockets. I couldn't bear the thought of them dropping me off at home, as Willem's mother had suggested.

His sister ogled me over her plate.

"Katrien, don't forget to eat," her mother said, with a smile. "Just let our friend here get on with it, will you."

They were kind to me, wanted me to feel at home. My unease was palpable, it was in my clothes, my checked shirt, my V-neck jumper, my knee socks. Nothing seemed to match, especially in comparison with the sleek, dark colours they all wore. They talked about travelling and the countryside of Spain. The names of towns flowed from their lips like magical formulas. When the subject of school came up, Willem's father raised his index finger and gave an imitation of the principal, "Mr Bouillie is a good man, Willem. A good man."

I joined in their laughter but didn't dare say very much, for fear that my attempts at polite conversation would remind them of the dank smell of bricks, moss and the walls of our cellar.

At home we did not talk much during meals. There were a few times when Roland rambled on about what he and his mates had been up to in class, making him choke with laughter, but mostly we all kept quiet.

We were Callewijns. We huddled together, we kept to ourselves behind the walls of the old farmhouse which in turn huddled against the dyke. At the sound of a strange car rumbling over the cobbles or reversing by the gate, or when unexpected visitors came to the door, we would all jump up and look out the window.

"I'll draw a picture of someone on the wall, shall I, then I'll have someone who'll listen to me," my mother often complained when there was no response to her list of chores that needed doing. We went through life with our fists clenched, for fear of being whisked away or robbed.

*

"I see you've made your bed for once," Willem's mother remarked.

He bent his head, pressing his chin on to his breast. His face reddened, and I could tell he was angry, not ashamed. When he got really wound up he would jiggle his knees. He did it in class, too, for no apparent reason, when we were given mathematical problems to solve and had to concentrate in stuffy silence. I could sense his anger in the air, which seemed to thicken around him.

It happened when he noted that Mr Bruane had found another victim to humiliate and at the sight of Mr Bouillie patrolling the yard, but it was most likely to happen during Mr Vaneenooghe's lessons, when he droned on and on about God, the Most High, in whose almighty machinery we were like grains of sand being ground to dust by sheer tedium.

They made fun of things at his house. My father wasn't good at that. The only mockery we had was my mother's. It propped her up, whereas my father was forever buckling. He would buckle under loads of grain or divine blessing, in the eyes of his foreman or those of Christ the King, who sat above the altar in church holding the globe of his creation amid the seraphim.

In the café he was eyed with the same sense of mild misgiving as I was beginning to feel more and more strongly when I looked at him, although I felt sadness as well. My father, a traitor to his farming stock. He didn't own any cattle, he had taken a job, he was just an ant in an army of workers. He drew up his shoulders and carried on in the countenance of the Lord.

I sensed condescension in the principal's attitude to me. Behind his dainty gold-rimmed spectacles his eyes told me that I was an ant like my father, not without talent, not a bad student, but still an ant with a father who had no money. Ant-hood was all I was good for. I would slave like an ant at maths and grammar, I would study the geographical distribution of industries in Belgium and also its natural resources, the products of which I would find myself carting about in later life, pouring into troughs, watching as they vanished into mills, just like my father.

*

I left the table before the pudding to go to the lavatory. Willem and his sister were having an argument and their father made a joke to stop them. I lowered the lid on the toilet and sat down with my elbows on my knees, trembling, and stayed there, staring at the door, until my breathing returned to normal.

At about three the weather cleared up. Willem's mother went off to drive his sister to her music lesson. His father vanished upstairs to his office.

We slouched in front of the television, watching a film in which knights in armour jousted. When the children's programme began I said I ought to be getting home. My trousers were dry. I took off the pair Willem had lent me and put mine on again. He grabbed me by my hips, hoisted me up and spun round until we both collapsed on his bed.

Next thing I knew we were wrestling, although it wasn't really wrestling. His fingers sought out places that I preferred to ignore, unless it was the dead of night and I was safely under the covers, for only then did I dare to read them like Braille.

I pushed him away, but not very forcefully. I could smell his hair as he lay back on top of my chest, and then, suddenly, I swore and threw him off me.

He did not get up from the bed, just said, "See you tomorrow," in an offhand way.

*

As usual I stopped in the middle of the bridge over the railway. The sky was still leaden. The church spire pierced the overhanging clouds, gauging their thickness. The bridge shook when the express train to Bruges thundered past beneath me.

I had the feeling I was somehow born to observe other people wallowing in riches of which they were quite unaware, and which would remain hidden from me in dark closets, on shelves that were far too high. I would only catch crumbs, coffee beans, alms, collecting them in tins, counting the times something struck the bottom, before sealing them up.

It was drizzling again. Great scrims of rain slid across the horizon.

Back home it would smell of cold and damp. Of my father's feet. Of the savoury steam curling up from the pans on the range and condensing on the ceiling. I would kick off my shoes, hang my dripping coat on the peg and go straight up to my room without saying a word, so I could pull the drawstring of our safe, stifling nest around me nice and tight.

I swallowed my cares, took a running jump and gave a shout as I sailed down the slope towards home.

CHAPTER 8

M Y BIRTHDAY CAME and went without a fuss. Coffee
for three, cake, no candles. We celebrated in silence:
my father, my mother and me. They had bought me a book:
Iceland, Child of Fire. They must have found it difficult to make
a choice from the shelves in the shop at Ruizele, or perhaps
elsewhere. Books with only words from beginning to end made
them wary—you never knew what might be in there—but
they knew I wasn't keen on picture books. Pictures belonged
in comics, and I had stacks of those.

I dare say they'd had some assistance from the bookseller,
who would have seized this opportunity to flog some leftover
stock while making a show of being polite and helpful. The
book he recommended had a few photographs in it, so at least
they had some idea of the contents, and I could imagine his satisfaction as he showed them out and watched them head across
the square to their car, relieved and happy with their purchase.

It was wrapped in brown paper. To brighten up the parcel
my mother had written "*Happy Birthday*" on it in her old-
fashioned florid script, followed by "*many happy returns of the
day. Ma & Pa.*"

Many happy returns. I had taken the book upstairs to my
room to look at. The taste of the kisses I had given to express

my gratitude was still on my lips, and my chest felt tight with the gloom that filled me as I climbed the stairs.

The book did not grab me. Not many things grabbed me nowadays. I had left it open on the table where I did my homework, so it looked as if I couldn't get enough of it, they'd ask how I liked it and I'd nod and say "it's great", but what I really wanted to do was stick it on the shelf along with the other books, which seemed to be closing ranks on me, keeping their stories from me and making my head swim with letters and punctuation marks instead.

*

Fourteen. I wrote the number down on a piece of paper and held it up to the light. I gazed at my reflection in the window pane, which was milky-white with mist. I didn't look fourteen. I ought to be wearing jeans and my hair in a fringe, I ought to go off on sailing trips with my friends the way the boys did in my adventure stories. They rode horses, too. During seaside holidays they thwarted the evil intentions of gangsters, survived shipwrecks and washed up on desert islands. There were ruined castles and bottomless pits. They hunted and found worm-eaten treasure chests filled with gold bars, rescued the daughters of business tycoons from remote fishing huts, and usually had a dog called Soda or maybe Tarzan, which could be relied on to give the game away by barking at the wrong moment. I couldn't have cared less about that stuff.

So they got to me in the end—the priest, Mr Bouillie and all the other staffroom creeps. A whole school year had passed, a summer had lit up and been snuffed out again, and I hadn't even noticed. At this rate it wouldn't be long before

I fell asleep altogether. Then, when I woke up again I'd be just like Roland. I'd lure new boys behind the cherry laurel and send them packing a few minutes later with tears in their eyes, having done goodness knows what to them, I'd punch people left and right and my halting voice would become a growl, I'd be good at football and get flustered when Roswita cheered me for being a fine runner.

His bed had not been slept in for several nights. He was staying with his parents for the half-term holiday. His mother was on leave from the institution everyone was so secretive about. There was the same sense of mystery surrounding the postcard she had sent from there, elegantly phrased in French but containing several spelling mistakes.

My father had said, "He's a poor sod, Roger is," and sighed heavily. My mother.

*

They called from the bottom of the stairs that they were going to visit the graves. It was November, and the mist would be catching on the chrysanthemums in the cemetery and making them soggy.

I stayed at home, lounging on my bed, flicking through exercise books and drawing monsters in the margins. Willem was away on a trip to the mountains with his parents, which he'd been greatly looking forward to. He couldn't wait to get away.

For all our efforts to look as if we were chewing the cud like the rest of them, our contrariness did not fail to attract attention, and there were moments when he too lost his cool, especially on the day we were summoned to the principal's office during break. Hardly an embodiment of divine authority in his bespoke suit, yet he exuded the stony severity of the Ten Commandments. A barely perceptible wrinkle played on his brow that afternoon as he sat himself down between the two of us on the leatherette couch. He fiddled with his tie pin, clasped his hands and looked grave.

"Gentlemen," he began.

"Yes, Father?"

I sensed the superior, measured scorn that was spreading through Willem, but at the same time I couldn't help feeling he was on his guard. The way he leaned back in the fake smell of the couch was a touch too devil-may-care, as was the relaxed expression on his face while he listened to the priest's obscure discourse on the subject of community spirit.

School did not minister to individual needs, those of individual boys in this case, it was best compared to a busy beehive. We were not to view our teachers—benign, devoted souls to a man—as our masters, but as older brothers who wanted only what was best for us. Mr Bouillie felt the same. The priest rambled on about the pillar of our establishment shedding bitter tears on our account, so much did it pain him that certain boys never showed up for extracurricular games or sport on Wednesday afternoon, that they never volunteered for dish-washing service, nor did their bit to keep the library open on Tuesdays, let alone on Fridays from four to six p.m.

"You want to be more outgoing, the pair of you. Do you understand what I'm saying? At your age... sticking together all the time... And there is so much more beauty and wisdom waiting to be discovered out in the world. Look, we're human, all of us… so am I," he said, pausing for emphasis. "You are young. Young and inexperienced, and the pure bond of friendship is a thing of great value, but still…"

It was as though he had hinges in his body that needed oiling. Doors were scraping over floors and getting jammed halfway, and he couldn't bring himself to force them open with a thrust of his shoulder.

"We all have strong feelings at times. And when one is young one is extra susceptible. Let's see, a fitting metaphor would be…"

He selected a Havana from the cigar box on his coffee table, lit it and balanced it on his lower lip, thought hard, blew out little puffs of smoke, and embarked on an ethereal parable about the light of love and flowers in bud needing time to unfold their petals, and what a shame it would be to disturb this tender process in any way. Of course, we were young and feckless, he had been young himself, and no less mischievous than us… It would be a pity if our high spirits caused us to nip each other in the bud.

I hadn't a clue what he was getting at, but I heard a little snort escape from Willem's nostrils. His cheekbones flushed briefly, from shame or anger I could not tell. He was certainly not jiggling his knees.

"So much for that, then," the priest said at last.

He gave us each a manly slap on the thigh and rose to his feet. "I know you're good boys at heart…"

He accompanied us into the corridor, visibly relieved at having acquitted himself of what must have been a delicate task.

Just before starting across the school yard, Willem turned round—he seemed to have been waiting for this moment—and told the priest that his father had said he'd be getting in touch soon, something about the spring fund-raising dinner for the purchase of two new vaulting horses for the gym.

"Yes indeed, we must see to that," replied the priest. "The poster has to go to the printer's. I'll ring him myself." His tone was level, but for some reason Willem's remark had touched a raw nerve.

We returned to the classroom. The bell for the end of break had already sounded, the yard was deserted.

"What was that all about?" I asked.

He just grinned and jostled me up the stairs. Everyone stared when we arrived in class.

*

After the summer holidays we were no longer in the same class. Without his presence the lessons became compact eternities. Boredom coiled itself around my neck like a thick scarf being pulled tight, throttling me slowly. I yearned for the four o'clock bell, yearned to go and wait for him on the edge of the wood, but in the meantime I had to struggle to stay awake in ever deeper dungeons of apathy, stealing looks out the window at the cavalries of clouds breaking ranks and straggling across the horizon, their lances broken and their banners torn to shreds; or glancing round the classroom at the others, all of them busy taking notes and shooting their hands up imploringly as soon as the teacher asked a question, at which my facial muscles would go rigid with contempt.

I'd have spat out the whole world and all the doomed creatures with it, including myself, if I'd been able, like getting rid of a gob of phlegm. I longed to be little again, when I was no more than a membrane upon which the days tapped their tattoo of impressions for me to take or leave. The days of screaming for my milk, and yawning. Going to sleep and waking up. Feeling the blaze of summer in my legs, lifting a tile in the cellar and discovering a salamander underneath, licking its chops like a dragon, then quickly dropping the tile back in place and running away crying, "Papa, Papa!" After dusk, when a hush descended on the outdoor world, there'd be the Aunts indoors, spreading their bats' wings and detaching themselves from the corners where they spent their days upside down and fast asleep, and I'd salute the sweetness of the night as it deepened into black, as black as the pages in the photograph albums which preserved my image under a sheet of tissue paper.

I thought of my father and my mother. His creations: man and woman. He read the paper, she did the dishes. She complained, he soothed. The sexes are complementary, but different, Mr Vaneenooghe had explained in class, and he had written the word on the blackboard: com-ple-men-tary. The story of the Creation revealed a profound truth, he had declared in conclusion, but I remained unconvinced.

His rusty-brown sweater and speckled jacket seemed to belie his words, for they hinted that his own better half vacuumed him twice a week along with the carpets, or laid him out on the wet grass to air. His tone turned melancholy when he alluded to the blessings of the family or to his own fatherhood and offspring. He had a boy and girl, whose names were Bjorn and Tineke. His own Christian name was Didier, which was bad enough.

With a view to adding what he liked to think of as a "personal note" to his lesson, he had come to class equipped with a wedding photograph of his own. His bride wore a beribboned cartwheel hat which hid most of her face. They posed side by side in front of a Japanese cherry tree, his arm round her waist, and he reminded me of a diminutive male spider mounting its gigantic mate. It was a colour photograph, but the colours were blighted with a purply sheen. No doubt it was kept on a window sill, where it would be taken up and contemplated routinely, until it was time to mow the lawn or wash the car.

"*The wedding will take place on October 4th,*" it said on the card stuck in my parents' leather-bound wedding album with silk tassels. Wedlock. A parcel of land enclosed by white picket fencing. No grass, just earth neatly divided into beds with leeks or haricot beans. Husband and wife having breakfast in the gazebo with its slender pillars and climbing roses. There's toast and jam, a brand-new tea cosy, Boch porcelain and Aunt Françoise's not very nice but very expensive tablecloth. When the sun has set and the screens are placed before the windows to keep the mosquitoes out, they'll enact the candlelight shadow-play which Mr Vaneenooghe said was at the heart of the bond between man and his helpmate, they'll find fulfilment in one another as creatures of flesh and blood, as the divine confirmation of love in life and death, which, he assured us—and I tried hard not to think of his whiskers—was as delicious as strawberries with whipped cream in a blizzard of caster sugar.

His lecture left us somewhat nonplussed. The rest of the lesson was devoted to studying Genesis Chapter Two, Verses eighteen to twenty-five. Mr Vaneenooghe sat down at his desk, reached a hand into his trousers and scratched his crotch at length.

At home it was raining bills that couldn't be paid. They spent long hours every evening fretting over household expenses, adding and subtracting, deciding against repair of the gutters in favour of someone they knew who knew about fridges and didn't charge too much, who poked around with screwdrivers and pliers and in the end got the thing going again, although it made such a racket you could hear it streets away.

I gritted my teeth. What did God care about love? He parted seas and burned cities to the ground, set armies upon each other like termites, laid wagers and cast lots for his own son's robe. He held our souls up to the light as if they were holiday slides, thrilling to the multitudinous patterns of our sins. On Ash Wednesday he made the sign of the cross on my forehead with grimy thumbs, whispering that I was a little heap of ashes mixed with water, and at the end of the lesson, when the others trooped out into the yard and I was kept in to clean the blackboard, my nostrils would sting with a smell like bad breath. I gazed out over the deserted desks, the satchels resting against the legs, the rulers, pens and pencils in the trays. I heard the clamour in the yard and was glad I had to stay in, even if it meant not seeing Willem. I soaked sponges, wiped them across expanses of blackboard, rose up on my toes, opened windows and knocked the chalk-dust out of dusters.

When the wind blew in from the west, which it nearly always did, half the dust blew back into my face, powdering me as white as the walls with their pockmarks indicating where pictures had hung until they fell down or were removed or shot down with rubber bands.

I screwed up my eyes. It got under my fingernails, in the

corners of my mouth, made me blink. It clogged up my nose, gave me an itchy feeling in my neck and made my hands dry. When I licked my fingers they no longer tasted of me. I am nothing, nobody, I thought. I belong nowhere, and everywhere. At last I was at one with the Holy Father.

CHAPTER 9

B Y MID-DECEMBER the frost had set in. It came with the irresistible clarity of an illusion, transforming tussocks of grass into spun sugar, etching trails of seaweed on the window pane, bearding the rafters in the attic with white stubble.

The days, frozen solid, were filleted by razor-sharp sunbeams and tinkled like little slivers of crystal.

It was summer the other way round. August in December, so bitingly cold at night that the sheets stung all my pores, obliging me to lie absolutely still, almost without breathing, until my body warmed them up. The slightest movement of an arm or a foot meant exchanging Africa for the North Pole.

We ran short of blankets. There were three or four on each bed, and still we shivered. It was so bad that Roland didn't protest when I gathered up my covers and slipped into bed beside him without even asking permission.

He turned over on his side to make room for me. I snuggled up to him, absorbing his body-heat like a sponge, listening to him go back to sleep, staring at the window and the icy, liana-infested night beyond.

We rolled against each other in the dip of the mattress. He slipped an arm under his pillow, my head lolled against his shoulder and I reeled from the scent of him. He turned over. We lay back to back. His spine rubbed against mine. We turned over again, twisted away from each other and tumbled back like dice, each time in a different combination. Front to back. Back to front. Front to front. We pulled the sheet up over our heads. It slipped down, and our necks were nipped by the cold. We burrowed under again, into the warmth.

I listened to him making nibbling sounds in his sleep, smacking his lips, mumbling incomprehensibly, and I could feel his fingers twitching fitfully. A tremor passed through his legs from time to time, and his head jerked on his pillow. What he was dreaming of, I imagined, would be a fair reflection of his day-to-day world, complete with straight chalked lines and goalposts and him kicking in, heading the ball, scoring goals.

Sleep came over me in waves, surging and ebbing by turns until I was swept away at last into dreamy warm currents beneath a cover of pack-ice. Cloud formations in the water. White tunnels filled with diffuse grey light. The green of algae. An almost palpable silence.

My dreams were seldom about familiar things now. Mostly they featured vast plains scattered with boulders, or streets in anonymous cities, square windowless towers with machines throbbing inside, steel gates sliding open for me to step into galleries with display cases filled with mineral specimens or stuffed birds.

There were dreams in which I sat at the garden table under the beech tree reading fat books which made my head swim with words, images, and ideas of an awe-inspiring, glorious logic. Connections, explanations so lucid, so precise, that I kept telling myself, even as I was reading: I must remember this! But before I could do so the sentences seemed to dissolve. My voice wavered. The words slipped away faster and faster

131

under my frantic gaze, blurring and sinking into the paper as I flipped through the pages.

I was startled awake by the heaving mattress. Roland was lying at the very edge of the bed, gasping for breath as if he had raced up ten flights of stairs.

I called his name. He responded with a sigh of exasperation.

He got out of bed, wrapped himself in a blanket and went downstairs.

I don't know how long he was gone, whether it was fifteen minutes or an hour. When he returned he smelled of mown grass. His forehead and his chest were beaded with sweat. He nestled himself languidly against me and the next instant he was asleep.

*

Morning came with a snowball splattering against the window, and my father calling us from outside, "Wakey wakey, lie-a-beds. Time to get up."

Huddled in our blankets, we crept downstairs like caterpillars. My father had disconnected all the taps upstairs, he had poked a torch under the floorboards to locate the mains, which branched out into pipes intersecting with others, vanishing into walls and reappearing in the most unlikely places.

Downstairs the kettle sang on the stove. A woman's voice on the radio burbled on about the country coming to a standstill, the King being struck down by the flu, railway points freezing in the tracks, harbours turning into glass, weights and measures going haywire and the Stock Exchange being in crisis. There was to be no pigeon racing, all sporting events had been cancelled, and the Minister of Education had ordered the schools to be closed throughout the country because heating was too expensive. The holidays were to be prolonged for another week.

My spirits soared. No school for a whole week.

"It's bitterly cold out," my father said, rubbing his hands as he came into the house. Yet outside it looked like summer, for the wind had blown drifts of white-hot dunes where the fields used to be.

"One really good snowfall a year is just fine by me," my mother said.

A blanket of snow invariably put her in a good mood. The world would be granted absolution, it would be pure again for as long as the weather lasted. I tried not to think of the slush, later on, when the thaw came and spoiled everything, and our shoes would go mouldy.

We were eating in silence when the telephone rang.

My father went out to the passage, returned after a few minutes and said, "It's for you."

I put down my fork and got up.

It was Willem.

"Fancy going skating?" he said.

*

His father drove him to our house. I was relieved to hear the car pull away after stopping by the gate.

My mother had spluttered at first, but my father said the ice was at least twenty centimetres thick, "Good, clean ice," he said. "The very best. And Roland should join the lads."

The wind had blown the snow against the dyke in banks, leaving a winding path in between. All we had to do was go down the dyke, cross the towpath and find a suitable place to step on the ice.

We put on thick Norwegian socks, thick sweaters, mittens and woolly hats with ear flaps. There were plenty of skates for us to choose from. At the back of a cupboard in one of the rooms there were several pairs jumbled together, some of which were wooden with blades you sharpened by hand. They had a nice curl at the ends, but the wood was badly mildewed.

As we were leaving the gate armed with a couple of potato sacks for us to sit on while we tied our skates, we caught sight of someone riding a bicycle towards us, wobbling because of the icy road, and waving one arm.

An Arab or a Laplander, or so it seemed. Turbaned, with a pom-pom bobbing up and down. It turned out to be Roswita.

"Well," Roland muttered. "I asked her to come."

She had left her retinue of girlfriends behind. She had been attending an expensive school in town for some time, where she had probably found herself a new bevy of admirers. Only rarely did she show up at choir practice these days, but she never missed a football match.

Townie words and expressions were creeping into her speech.

"What a drag," she would say, when Mr Snellaert made us rehearse the same chorus for the sixth time.

She also said she did Latin, which she pronounced with a frivolous little aspiration of the t—not that she was keen on all those ancient Romans, mind. When someone told her a joke she no longer laughed, she didn't even pretend to be amused, she just said, "Hey, you don't say,"—whatever that was supposed to mean.

She took her skates out of the carrier on her bike. "It's been ages," she said. "I've probably lost the knack."

"Don't worry," Roland replied. "I'll help you."

It was his misfortune that his voice still switched from deep to an embarrassing squeak at times, especially when, as now, he was putting on a display of superiority. He pretended not to hear it himself, but his cheeks betrayed him.

I could tell that Willem was just as amused as I was, but neither of us let on.

"Who's he?" Roswita asked, when Willem and Roland went on ahead to look for a less snowbound spot.

"He's in my class. His Pa's an architect."

She had already looked him up and down appraisingly, I couldn't help noticing, and no doubt decided that he was too young, too timid or too distant for her wiles, but mention of the word "architect" had made her look again.

"Does he do all right at school?"

"Not bad."

The others were already on the ice.

"Come on, you lot," Roland called, "if I have to stand here much longer my cock'll freeze off."

It was one of those typical things he'd come up with when he was embarrassed or flustered and said stuff I thought was crude, or stupid, or both.

"Why don't you give me a hand," Roswita called back at him. "Instead of playing the fool."

One of her skates got caught on a reed stalk and I saw the crotch of the knitted pants she wore over her tights. Roland made a great fuss of patting the snow off her pleated skirt.

We glided past the warehouses, under the bridge, where the landscape was still empty and open. I had the feeling that I suddenly had an awful lot to say. Everyone else always seemed to be yakking non-stop, in the refectory, in class, in the yard, in the market square after school. About stickers and cars. About the girl with the blonde hair, or the other one, with plaits—pity about all those freckles.

All that left me cold. Him too. He had books about ducks. About the jungle in Brazil. Anacondas. Mount Everest. I could have told him all about *Iceland, Child of Fire*, but I still hadn't read it. Or about the first time I was taken to the seaside where, so my mother told me for I was too young to remember, I was so horrified by the sand that I hadn't stopped bawling all day. The second time I had been bitterly disappointed that I couldn't see America across the water, whereas in my atlas all the continents seemed so reassuringly close together. I could have told him that I sometimes wondered whether the solar system might be an atom. It was possible, I thought. The question intrigued me, more anyway than the Newtonian mumbo-jumbo Father Buyl distributed from behind his battery of lenses and mirrors like dry biscuits for our consumption.

I had thought about it long and hard. The possibility that I myself might consist of an infinite number of solar systems— and within one a planet like ours, and on one of its continents someone like me, but with any luck happier than me, which I would certainly be if there weren't any schools—had made me even more doubtful about what God was up to.

"It's nice here," said Willem.

I looked up. Nice wasn't the word for the world that had enfolded me from the cradle on. Whenever I stepped out of the gate a feeling of forlornness would creep over me. It wasn't just the warehouses draping their wobbly reflections in the water, blotting out my memories like an irritating ink stain. It wasn't that there was too much sky, either, not even on the far side of the canal where there were no trees to relieve the starkness. Since starting my new school I sometimes felt as if I were surveying my surroundings through the wrong end of a telescope, and on other days through a microscope. The narrowness, the forsakenness of it all did not escape me, and I felt suffocated and deserted by turns.

"It's because of the snow," I said.

He didn't agree. It was because of the slope upon which Zomergem was situated, that was what made the view interesting. We were at the lowest point of the Flemish lowlands. He had a book about the region.

We heard a shriek behind us. Then the sound of someone crashing into the brittle reeds by the bank, and Roswita railing against Roland for not being careful.

"Let's turn round and go back," I said. "Then we can go a bit further in the other direction." We were already quite far from home, and I had spotted a couple of other skaters in the distance. I had no desire to join them.

He glided to an unsteady halt. I was the better skater. He had trouble keeping his balance, seemed unused to his own height.

For a while the only sound was the crunch and swish of our skates and Roland circling round Roswita, pushing her from behind, letting her go, skating off and returning at full speed to push her again.

She screamed.

He put his hands on her hips and braked.

They huddled together, talking in low voices and throwing quick glances in our direction.

Then he grabbed her hand and pulled her away with him. "We're going to Bruges!" he shouted over his shoulder.

She begged him to slow down.

He wouldn't listen.

"They're heading for a fall," Willem said.

They fell. It was Roswita who lost her balance first, stumbled, flailed her arms and clutched at his sweater as she fell, so that his foot shot away and he crashed on to the ice on his side.

The ice groaned. I could feel a tremor under my feet. Jagged cracks shot across the frozen canal. We held our breath.

Roland scrambled to his feet and stood there, rubbing his shoulder, dismayed. Roswita was stuck in a bank of snow. She wouldn't let him help her.

"I can get up by myself. I want to go back."

"I'm sorry sweetie," I heard him say. "I'll take you home, all right?"

*

Towards the end of the afternoon the clouds gathered again. The sun was a watery orange blob sinking fast. The wind rose.

My mother offered us hot chocolate and raisin bread. The light was already fading and Roland still hadn't returned. She was getting worried.

"He's old enough to look after himself," my father said. "He knows what he's doing."

"Have you had enough? Would you like anything else?" he asked Willem.

"I'm fine, thank you."

"Will they be coming to fetch you?"

"Yes, at about seven."

My mother glanced furtively at her watch. "Now, where can he have got to?"

He did not arrive until eight.

"I hung around for a bit," he muttered. "And we had to shelter."

He was deathly pale, and his legs were shaking.

"See a ghost on the way, by any chance?" my father asked. "You're as white as a sheet…"

Roland sat down at the table.

"No," he said, "worse than that."

My father gave a short laugh.

Not long afterwards, maybe a quarter of an hour, the phone rang. My father answered it.

"Ours has conked out too," I heard him say. "The anti-freeze isn't strong enough to deal with this kind of weather… No, never mind… We'll think of something… No problem. I'll get him…"

"It's your Pa," he told Willem. "His car's broken down. Mother, we have a guest for the night."

"Well, I hope I've got enough bedding," she replied.

*

After supper Roland went straight upstairs. My father remained seated at the table for quite a while, chatting to us. He didn't usually talk much, but when he did he would talk in bursts. He wanted to seize the fullness of past summers before it slipped like sand through his fingers. I could sense the images flitting across his retina, of trees in the orchard cut down years ago, and of the garden in its prime. The garden, which was so vast that you could get lost in it. That was when he was a boy, when in the summer holidays his mother would pack a surprise picnic for the children to take on their exploring expeditions round the world that existed within the confines of the farm.

My mother joined us. "I've had to use a tablecloth as a bottom sheet," she said. "Not ideal, I know, but it's got a pretty floral pattern."

"Can't tell the difference in the dark anyway," Willem said.

I hoped she wouldn't start telling him about me. She would do that occasionally—go off at a tangent about how she'd tried breastfeeding me but had to give up after two weeks because I gave her a rash, which meant I was getting more blood inside me than milk. I was afraid this was going to be one of those occasions. She'd had a drink of gin and the stove was purring.

"His favourite place was his potty," she told Willem.

Here we go, I thought.

"He could spend hours on it, quite happily. If he was any trouble, all I had to do was sit him on his potty. And he's still the same, really…" she giggled.

"Ma!"

"It's true isn't it? Reading the paper on the lav. Just like your Pa, you are…"

"I do that too, sometimes," Willem said pleasantly.

He could tell I was ashamed of her. "I'd better be getting to bed," he said.

"Anton will show you the way."

*

My mother had prepared one of the old spare rooms. It must have been years since it had last been used. It smelt a bit stuffy, and it was freezing cold in there. She had laid an old sleeping bag on the bed as extra blanket.

Willem put his hands in his pockets. I noticed him shivering.

"It's all a bit makeshift here," I said apologetically.

"It's fine."

"If you're cold you must say so. I can get you an extra pullover."

"I'll be all right."

"Night," I said.

"Night."

*

I came upon Roland in the bathroom, inspecting the inside of his lower lip in the mirror.

"Did you hurt yourself?"

"No, no," he said quickly. "I just bit my tongue, that's all."

I started brushing my teeth.

He held his head under the tap and dried himself with a towel.

"Right, see you in the morning."

"See you."

Everyone had gone upstairs. All the lights were out. The stove was still warm, and I sat down in the dark.

I didn't feel sleepy, I never did when it snowed. This was a throwback to when I was little, when I waited for weeks for the snow to arrive, and when it came at last I'd slip out of bed at night and cross to the window to check whether I could still see the flakes falling in the cones of light cast by the street lamps on the dyke road.

The wind buffeted the walls. The limbs of the beech tree tapped against the shutters. I remembered the cosiness that went with stormy weather in the old days, when I'd struggle to stay awake as long as I could so I'd feel safe all through the night.

Someone came down the stairs. I could hear bare feet thumping on the treads.

"Anton?"

"Over here," I said.

"I couldn't find you anywhere."

He hopped from one foot to the other. "Where's the toilet down here?"

"Sorry," I said, "Down the passage, turn right, it's the second door."

He padded out of the room.

Another six days or so and I'd sink back into boredom again. The idea paralysed me. Sometimes it started on the Saturday morning, when the prospect of having to get on my bike to undergo dreary lessons, teachers, discipline, being spied on and humiliated all over again would put me in a bad mood all weekend. School and I were not meant for each other. I simply did not exist. Just some little runt in cheap clothes, bought so I could grow into them, and I was tolerated because I behaved myself, because I let them ram all their lessons down my throat so I could cough them up again when required, but in reality they trusted me as little as I trusted them, and there were no generous donations from my father to make up for it.

I noted his crossword lying on the table, my mother's copy of the Women's Union magazine with free knitting patterns, the unopened envelopes behind the clock on the mantelpiece, and became acutely aware of the house that was home: dilapidated, old, emptier than ever.

The wind seemed to be digging out the foundations and lifting up the walls. The notion came as a relief. If only I myself could blow away in the wind like a lost letter fluttering across the fields, and once the thaw set in I'd let all my garbled sentences and nonsensical words leak away into the melted snow. I was reminded of the time in class when we were given yet another form to fill in and I simply put a tick in the box next to the word "born", whereupon Mr Vaneenooghe gave me extra homework for punishment, although it made perfectly good sense to me.

I heard a door opening behind me and falling to.

"In one of your moods again, are you," Willem said.

He lolled against the back of my chair.

"I know. I'm a pain sometimes."

"Who isn't?"

I said nothing.

"C'mon. Let's go to bed."

I stayed where I was.

He slipped his hands under my collar and leaned forward.

PART III

CHAPTER I

Paris. Soissons. Senlis. Summer 197*, the last school trip before our final exams and going off to university. Pointed arches, triforia, triptychs. Willem leaping in front of my camera lens going *boo*, time after time. Me pretending to be annoyed by his tomfoolery and striding ahead to stay close to our guide. I was going to study history, and didn't want to miss anything. He found it all very boring and would duck into niches to pose among statues of prophets or ape the attitudes of martyrs and holy virgins. Not once did I press the shutter.

Nearly nineteen. When I try to recall the way I was then, with my long hair and the long white shirts I wore loose and flowing so they felt almost like a dress; when I look at old Polaroids of parties or outings and see that thin, lanky body harbouring passions that shattered like mirrors, shoulders invariably hunched, defensive, with Willem leaning against me, flaunting his beloved jangly armbands and necklaces, pulling faces and grinning and pointing his finger at the camera—what do I see? How can that be me?

He might have been my son, were he not one of the annual growth rings that have become ingrained in me along with what counts as "the past", in a blur solidifying by the day. I catch myself contemplating his likeness with the melancholy satisfaction of a father observing his child, still young enough to enjoy simple, frivolous pleasures. Or should I not think of frivolity but of the unmitigated, boundless joys we thought would never end, even as time was grinding us down?

You can already tell where the first lines will be etched around the eyes. Lurking at the back of the smile, wide and angular, which seems almost to tear the face in two, there is already a hint of the grief that will come back like a boomerang to collar him as he hears himself roaring with laughter and thinks: here I am, I'm having a good time, life is being kind to me.

That apparently inescapable footnote of sorrow, chasing each moment of pleasure more doggedly year by year, sometimes hard on the heels, sometimes at a discreet distance—where does it come from? A tap on the shoulder from the dead, maybe, which I never felt when I was young and feckless. There, far away on the horizon, waving their black handkerchiefs, the dead stand out ever more sharply against the sky.

Perhaps it has something to do with the feeling that everyone in the pictures is dead. Not just the sense of unreality and emptiness that fills me as I go through old photographs and come upon myself at some party or other, engaged in animated conversation with someone whose existence has shrunk to a cardboard shape. It's also seeing myself holding a glass in mid-air, halfway between the table and my mouth. Or sitting on a bench in a park somewhere, looking up in the tender light of spring at whoever was with me at the time.

It needn't have been Willem who took that photograph. But the image has the elegant composition that seemed to come naturally to him, and there's the bird's eye perspective—a device he fancied. My face, all smiles, looks like the centre of a flower supported by the narrow stalk of my torso.

It can't possibly have been taken by Roland. Photography didn't interest him much, and the few times he did pick up a camera he managed to decapitate entire wedding parties at a stroke. He managed to slice me down the middle once, when I posed for him leaning against a tree.

He left school two years before we did. His results weren't brilliant, but they weren't bad either. He opted for a career in business, and from then on drifted from one branch of casual trade to the next: Oriental rugs, baby clothes, whirlpool baths, army surplus. The police were after him at one point and he kept having problems with customs inspectors, but he always managed to keep his head above water.

There must be pictures in the family albums of him wearing that slightly shady grin of his. Macho, square-jawed, hair cropped short. There's a snapshot of the day his mother came home: Roland resting both hands on the back of her chair, in her eyes the glazed look of the heavily sedated. Surrounded by family members wreathed in dutiful smiles, his mother gazes down at the enormous slice of cake on her plate as though dreading the prospect of having to eat it. Roland stands behind her, stooping slightly to form a sort of little roof to protect her, but at the same time his eyes are raised and seem to say, "Yes, this is my mother. This is the sad creature who bore me. Poor, dear, half-witted Mama. Just as well I'm not a softie, and there's still the inheritance to look forward to."

The tip of his tie—as a self-proclaimed whizz-kid he went around formally dressed in a suit and tie—rests on her shoulder, giving the picture an entirely fortuitous note of intimacy.

There were a few occasions, later on, when his visits to my parents coincided with mine, and each time, as I watched him lift his little daughters from the back seat of his car and open the boot to take out push chairs, bags with nappies and baby bottles, I felt a slight pang of disappointment. In the end he got himself a perfectly insulated house in one of the new settlements that were springing up around the old villages all over the country, the kind of place where the wind plays listlessly in acacia trees and scatters lawns with the resigned sort of happiness that cowers behind tall reed fences, for fear of getting hurt.

I don't enjoy coming face to face with myself in pictures of me with shoulders hunched, conversing with one of the many girlfriends he had over the years. A Lydia maybe, or a Natalie. Fair-haired or dark. Shy or rattling on and on like an alarm clock you couldn't switch off. Sometimes he'd bring a girl home with him to spend the night at our house. A better place for a shag, I imagine, than that gloomy villa his parents lived in. Although it was grand enough to impress his sweethearts, there was always the risk that his mother would spend half the night shambling up and down the corridor like a drugged bear or put the roast in the oven at half-past two in the morning.

Of the pain caused by the noises of his lust, the knife being twisted in the wound with every thrust of his body, there is no visual record. He was brimming with life. Alive in every fibre of his being, each gland in his body on the alert, a bundle of convoluted surfaces: lungs, gut, veins under the outer layer of skin. He drew the breath of life with workmanlike intent, drank it to the dregs, and belched. Life no longer slipped tormentingly through his fingers.

The human body does what it is programmed to do with quiet purpose, it brooks no contradiction. It grows, provides ready-furnished rooms for you to inhabit and make your own, whether you like them or not. Had he been punier, he'd have played the piano, loved Liszt and fought hard not to weep during the *Lacrimosa*. Had I been heftier, I'd have shot thrushes out of the cherry tree and wrung their necks when they fell to the ground, without flinching, just for the heck of it.

I remember the day he discovered a litter of kittens, a few weeks old. Cats were a plague in the empty stables. He smashed their skulls one by one with a heavy chisel. I turned away so as not to vomit. When it was all over he stood with bloody hands looking down at the mess of split skulls and bulging eyes without a trace of pity, rather with interest, as if this were just another demonstration of how little death meant.

One day he found a woodcock in the orchard, caught in a length of barbed wire. He spent the entire Wednesday afternoon searching cellars and pantries for a suitable bottle, and subsequently for a cork that fitted tight. He filled the bottle with sand and tied a piece of string around the neck at one end and around the bird's legs at the other, after which he made for the bridge over the canal.

When he got there he leaned over the railing and saluted as he dropped the bird into the water.

For the next few days he kept saying, "Must be rotting nicely down there. Unless the rats got to it first." The grim satisfaction in his voice sent shivers down my spine.

*

151

The older a photograph, the less familiar the people in it will appear, but for me, curiously enough, it works the other way round. Aunt Odette's albums—she was already pasting in photographs before my father was born—transport me directly to the frozen clamour of family gatherings long ago. Quite who is being congratulated or mourned in the shade of the beech tree, the same place where my father would set up the folding table when I was a boy, makes little difference. It is the same happiness, the same sorrow, passing through an ever-changing array of figures. Whether anniversary or funeral, whether the garden is festooned with flags or with black draperies, the lawn breathes the calm, domesticated atmosphere that goes with the dead long since laid to rest.

Dried edelweiss. Snow-capped mountains. Aunt Odette in a long dress by the lake at Geneva, brimming with expectations as yet unsoured. In Cologne, by the Cathedral, and on the steps of the Sankt Gereon as yet undevastated by war, carrying her jacket over her arm, her eyes shaded by the brim of her little hat.

The towers of Prague (a thousand times lovelier than Vienna) viewed from the Charles Bridge. The banks of the Vltava. Unter den Linden. The Champs Elysées. Standing by a hotel entrance, Aunt Odette looks happy, as though expecting the offer of a gentleman's arm. The motor cars she gets in and out of are benign, glossy beetles. Time seems to have been differently organised then, with minutes still being minutes, but in less of a hurry. The figures peopling those busy boulevards seem always to be strolling, heading nowhere in particular. Aunt Odette must have felt herself in an ocean of time, standing on the deck of a royal steamship without a single sandbank or iceberg in sight.

Here she has posted herself beside the front door, unaware of Flora and Alice in the doorway with their arms around each other, puffing up their cheeks and sticking out their tongues. The next snapshot shows her dismay at catching the girls poking fun at her. Then there is a third picture, in which the three of them pose side by side trying not to laugh, for being photographed was not to be taken lightly in those days.

*

In that final photo of us on the monastery steps, taken on the day our school diplomas were awarded, it is not as sunny as the day when my father posed there. Willem and I are both grinning from ear to ear.

Our collars itched. I felt I was being slowly throttled by my tie. The ceremony was accompanied by string music in the refectory. Our priestly principal was in such good humour that he resembled a well-fed blue tit fluttering this way and that on the podium, so beside himself with pride that he almost lost his balance.

One lad was taking mathematics at university, another would be reading economics. The priest fiddled blissfully with the lapels of his jacket, not without relief, I suspect, that the good name of the school had survived the year untarnished.

Mr Bouillie, in a rush of uncharacteristic geniality, proposed drinks at the Christian community centre on the square, for some man-to-man talk for a change. Willem and I did not join them. Directly after the official presentation we leapt on our bikes and made for the woods. We very nearly flung our diplomas into a ditch out of sheer bravado. To shed all excess baggage.

We soared in the June air. The caprices of spring were over. Now was the time for sprinklers tapping out their steady circular showers on rich people's lawns. Whooping for joy, Willem swerved crazily on his bike across the road in an attempt to force me into the verge.

Of the pair of us, I was the more dutiful. I was the one who stopped at crossroads, I hardly ever ignored a red light and always stuck out the correct arm to signal a left or right turn.

"Did you pass?" his mother cried from the carport when she heard us come in.

"Passed!" we shouted in unison.

Loud kisses were planted on our cheeks. Katrien came down briefly, a little downcast because she still had her piano exam to do later in the day. Arpeggios draped themselves like feather boas around our shoulders.

Out on the terrace, under the awning, Willem's father popped a bottle of champagne and raised his glass in a toast.

"Here's to our diploma!" Willem yelled. "To freedom!"

"And to the future," said his father.

History was certainly an interesting choice, everyone agreed, but the fact that Willem had chosen to study medicine made them visibly proud.

"I might even get rid of that ache in my shoulder," his mother joked.

"Not if it's cancer," Willem laughed, "I expect it's terminal."

Heady with wine, she gave him a few playful slaps, then made for the kitchen to baste her joint of beef.

*

We went to Ghent together to hunt for student lodgings. We were in this together, but not entirely. Willem thought we'd distract each other too much if we shared a flat. I was put out at first and then agreed with him.

We found a place for me in an old town house by the River Schelde, close by the university. The ground floor, a neo-baroque showcase stuffed with sombre armchairs, was the domain of the elderly landlady, Miss Lachaert, who seemed to be constructed of floor-sweepings tied together with a little apron of felt.

She circled all around me, shuffling in her quilted slippers, then put her enormous glasses on her nose and scrutinised me at length, as if my entire life were written in neat paragraphs across my forehead for her to read.

"No visitors after ten p.m.," she said finally. "And the first time you have female company will be the last."

"Have no fear, Madam," Willem said innocently. "He's far too serious for girls."

She handed over a key. Third floor, second door on the left, she told us.

The room was rather small, formerly occupied by domestic servants. The wallpaper was in the bold stripes of old-fashioned pyjamas, and you could tell by the stuffiness of the place that it would get very hot in summer. But I liked it. The window looked out on a bell tower from which a carillon pealed out every quarter hour.

There was a bathroom and a narrow kitchen which I was to share with the only other lodger, a student with greasy hair who sat like Samson between pillars of books, poring over his chemistry textbooks, and who barely raised his eyes in greeting. His room had the look of an underground lair in which he was hibernating on a permanent basis.

He wouldn't give me any trouble, that was clear.

"So this is to be our kingdom," Willem said.

"Is it to your liking?" a voice squeaked behind us. It was the landlady, who must have been following us the whole time in her inaudible slippers.

"It's fine!" I stammered. "Excellent, in fact."

She descended the stairs at a maddeningly slow pace and showed us out.

*

Willem found student lodgings in a modern residential hall situated at a busy crossroads. I couldn't have stuck it there for more than half an hour. The interior was regulation white formica all over the place. His room had two windows, beneath which there was the constant rumble of traffic. But you could see the hospital from it. Sitting at his writing table he had a view of the pavilions, the car park teeming with visitors, the small lawns dotted about where nurses or students stretched their legs and took off their shoes during the lunch hour.

Soon afterwards he left for the seaside, where he was to spend a month helping out at a pastry shop owned by an aunt. I visited him there on one of his few days off. We wandered up and down the tideline on the beach, rolled down dunes and built childish sand castles.

Up in the loft over the bakery stood his narrow bunk. He moved over to make room for me and curled his bony body around mine. I pricked myself on one of his earrings—his aunt wouldn't hear of him wearing "that junk" in the shop—and in the awkward entanglement that followed we tumbled off the bed. We held our breath, but the noise was followed only by silence. Clearly his aunt was not a light sleeper.

At the end of July he had to join his father and mother on a trip to Italy. "A tour of the palazzos," he said, wrinkling his nose. His father was the kind of tourist for whom world cities are life-size illustrations of a travel guide.

A postcard arrived from Verona, saying the weather was hot, that he wished I was there, that he was overdosing on pasta. We would meet again early in September, when the annual fair was held in Ruizele.

CHAPTER 2

T HE REST OF THE SUMMER was taken up with lounging about, packing my things and helping my parents
to move house, which they did slowly, bit by bit. The whole
place smelled of cardboard. There were boxes stacked up
like sarcophagi in every room.

My father was getting on for sixty and eligible for early
retirement. I think he was relieved to be spared the further
decay of the house he was born in, although our new home,
on a housing estate and the mirror image of the houses
across the road, must secretly have dismayed him as much
as it dismayed me.

At the end of August Roswita got married. I climbed up to
the rood-loft for my last performance as a chorister. Swathed
in raw silk, lace and tulle, she advanced towards the altar
down below, where a pale young man wearing a very wide
tie awaited her amid fountains of lilies.

The reception was held in her father's garden. In the
marquee she came up to me and asked how I was.

"Fine," I said. "Great, really."

We both glanced round, taking in the bobbing hats of the
ladies, their lavish frocks, the waiters hovering over the trays
of dressed lobsters on the terrace.

"History," she echoed, with a hint of awe in her voice, when I told her I'd be going to university. "Not my style. I was never one for learning. Can't sit still long enough." She smiled apologetically.

The bridegroom came towards us, inquired with whom he had the pleasure. Fortified by drink, he planted a fleeting kiss behind her ear and moved away.

"And how's Roland?" she asked.

"Haven't seen him for ages. He's working, and his mother's living at home again."

She nodded, peered down at her glass. We still felt awkward in each other's company. Observing her as she darted looks at the crowd, greeting people she knew with a little wave, I asked myself if this was a threshold for her: would she cross it and step out into the world or would it be a barrier that she'd welcome for its reassuring finality?

Dotted about the lawn were samples of every stage of her future. Children playing. Infants sated with cereal burping blissfully on their mothers' shoulders. Teenagers drinking themselves silly. Portly gentlemen and elderly ladies laden with jewellery, their faces bright pink from the holiday in Spain.

In forty or fifty years' time she'd be just like all those aunts and grandmothers gossiping in the shade of a pine tree, wearing hats designed to make up for lost youthful prettiness, and like them, barely recovered from a hip replacement, she'd hobble over to her grandchildren to pat them on the head.

I smiled at her sheepishly and said the champagne was very good.

She shrugged her shoulders. "You know my Pa. It's always nothing but the best for him."

Looking past her I spotted him heading towards us, waving his arm. At the foot of the terrace there was a rollicking crowd from the old football club, yelling "Long live love!" and to my shame, I couldn't help wondering how many of them had felt her up and groaned in the shadows of the castle drive. I pushed the thought away.

"Your father's looking for you," I said, just before he came up behind her and slipped his arm through hers.

She turned to me and waved. "See you later maybe."

"See you," I said. "Best of luck."

*

This was to be the last night I slept at home. I would be going to Ghent in the morning to settle into my student lodgings, and didn't intend to return until my parents had moved to the new house.

I took some soup bowls, cutlery, a few cups, and stacked them in a box.

Upstairs I heard the occasional argument.

"But Pa, we can't keep everything," my mother cried, and I could hear my father grumble in protest.

The room designated for the items of furniture that were no longer wanted filled up with heartache. Cupboards, cabinets and tables huddled together in docile anticipation of their second-hand fate.

Evening fell. The wind changed direction, and the cooling breeze made the house shrink audibly. The beech came alive as a late-summer flock of starlings settled in its branches, transforming the tree into a great music box pealing out an uninterrupted chorus of twittering and chirping. In the moonlight I could make out the birds among the foliage preening their feathers and squabbling over the prime perches. Now and then a contingent of them would detach itself soundlessly and alight in the gutter with a soft patter. Towards daybreak the concert would burst forth again, and with the first ray of sunshine the whole flock would whoosh up into the sky.

*

I drove to Ghent in my father's car with the back seat piled high with things for my student lodgings. I put up shelves for my books, unpacked my reading lamp, placed a stack of new paper in the drawer of my work table, and surveyed my new home with contentment. The window was open. In the courtyard of an adjacent building I glimpsed a girl in a run-down conservatory modelling something in clay; she had a cigarette in her mouth and the radio turned up full blast. Pigeons swooped around the bell tower. Trams jangled past in the street.

In the middle of the night I heard my fellow lodger crawl out of his burrow and scurry about in the kitchen. He put the kettle on. Soon afterwards he slunk back to his room, no doubt clutching a mug of hot coffee in his paws.

The next morning I went for a stroll downtown and ended up buying several things I didn't really need. A steel pepper mill with a long handle, for instance, and at the flea market I picked up a small shaving mirror and a few cups. There was an atmosphere of late-summer lethargy in the streets. In the September sunshine, already slanting and coppery, the streets seemed to be sleeping off the intoxication of summer.

I walked past the university buildings just to get a sniff of the place. There were students sitting on benches by the professors' offices, riffling through their textbooks. The plane trees at the entrance were shedding their first leaves.

I returned to my lodgings and had nearly reached the top of the stairs when a door opened in the hall downstairs and I heard the landlady's shuffling step.

"Your parents phoned," she called up to me. "You're to ring them right back."

I left my purchases on the stairs and came down, intending to go out and call from a phone box, but Miss Lachaert was holding the door of her parlour open for me and gesturing towards her telephone, which sat on an absurd pedestal beside the fireplace.

I lifted the receiver and dialled my parents' number. My father answered the phone.

"Bad news," he said.

His words didn't sink in. Miss Lachaert was hovering nearby, whisking her feather duster over picture frames and figurines to disguise her eavesdropping.

"I must go and see them," I told my father.

My mother called from the background, "He mustn't call on those people without changing into clean clothes. Pa, tell him he mustn't."

"I'll come and see you afterwards." I put the phone down before he could reply.

*

The bandstand on Ruizele's main square was occupied by a brass band playing Glenn Miller, and an evening market

162

was in full swing. A policeman was diverting the traffic. The high street was thronged with people and hooting cars. I rolled down the window, leaned back and waited. I felt the old resignation mixed with impatience, which I had grown so familiar with thanks to all that sitting around, waiting for Willem in the station restaurant or the café opposite the bus stop, where I'd listen to the buzz of voices and let my thoughts drift along with the waiters calling their orders to the kitchen, taking care not to keep glancing at the clock slowly ticking the seconds away and making me feel more lost than ever.

Families in their Sunday best squeezed past the bumpers of waiting cars. Boys on bicycles rode on the pavement, ringing their bells shrilly and braking suddenly when the traffic policeman signalled for them to dismount.

I clenched my fists round the driving wheel, steeled myself. All I could think of was that I had to see Willem, his father, his mother, all of them, and suddenly I was flooded with panic.

The policeman blew his whistle and spread his arms. The cars in front of me started to move.

I drove around the main square and away, up the hill, into the wood. I parked the car on the side of the road, walked up the drive to the front door framed in withering honeysuckle, and rang the bell.

Nothing happened.

I waited for a moment, rang the bell again and was already heading back to the car when someone called my name.

It was Katrien.

I turned round leadenly, at a loss for words to say to her, but she had vanished into the house, leaving the door open.

*

She was sitting in one of the leather armchairs by the big window, hugging her raised knees. The side table was littered with dirty cups around a tray of biscuits that had not been touched.

"They're not here," she said. "They left a while ago, with my aunt. I wanted to be alone."

"If you'd rather I came back another time," I mumbled.

Shaking her head, she tucked a lock of hair behind her ear. "It's all right."

She rose, thrust her hands into the pockets of her trousers and crossed to the window overlooking the lawn, the old climbing frame, the roly-poly woman doing her mindless dance.

"When did it happen?" I asked.

"Yesterday, around five. The police came round at half-past six."

She turned away from the window, started collecting the cups on a tray. "They're taking him to the mortuary tonight. I don't know how long they'll be."

She picked up the tray and went through to the kitchen. I heard her turn on a tap and rinse the cups.

I didn't dare stand up. Thoughts raced through my head, jostling and shouting to make themselves heard and bring me to my senses. He must have had a fall, nothing serious, or flown into a rage and slammed the door to the bathroom so hard that the key snapped off and now he's locked inside. He's run away from home. He's climbed to the top of a very tall tree and can't get down, so they need firemen with ladders to rescue him, but he clings to the branches, shouting, "Just leave me alone, the lot of you."

I fought back my tears and made for the kitchen, took a tea towel from the hook by the sink and started drying the cups.

"No need for that," Katrien said absently.

She was wearing her mother's bright-pink rubber gloves.

I watched her wash the saucers by turning them over and over in the dish water.

"Anton…"

"Yes?"

Her hands sank into the foam, groping for cutlery on the bottom.

"I've always known, you know."

I felt my stomach tighten, heard myself ask, stupidly, "What do you mean?"

"I'm not daft."

I took a cup from the draining board. "And them? What about them?" I asked, meaning her parents.

She paused, stared blankly at the pot of basil flowering on the window ledge above the tap.

"My mother, maybe. She always used to say, 'I can't make him out.'"

"Well, he did keep things to himself," I said.

A crooked smile crossed her lips. "She was referring to you."

Not knowing how to react to this, I held the cup up against the light as if it were a glass and asked, "When will it be?"

"Saturday most likely. They've got a lot of organising to do for the cremation."

She peeled off the pink gloves and took the cup from my hands.

"That'll do fine," she said, putting it away in the cupboard over the sink.

I leaned back against the kitchen table and covered my eyes with my hands.

She said my name. Her voice caught in her throat.

I heard her leave the kitchen.

When I had calmed down I found her back in the living room on the couch by the window.

"Sorry," I said.

She shook her head. Lit a cigarette. "Why don't you go upstairs."

I looked at her questioningly.

"Take something for yourself. Anything, doesn't matter what." She nodded towards the staircase.

*

The bedclothes were still rumpled, the pillow still faintly dented by his head. There was a kitschy Virgin Mary, a souvenir from Lourdes, with several of his bangles gleaming at the base. His wristwatch lay there ticking softly; he must have forgotten to wear it, as he so often did.

The carpet was strewn with two pairs of discarded socks, a couple of pairs of underpants and a vest, marking a trail from the bed to the laundry basket behind the door. On the desk by the window lay an open anatomy textbook. I clapped it shut.

Propped against the books on the shelves were snapshots of the summer camp where he'd flirted with a boy called Koen and where, on that last night by the farewell bonfire, he'd come on so strongly to some girl that she sent him perfumed letters every fortnight for months afterwards. The picture of our whole group at the foot of a dune shows me sulking. He roars with laughter, throws his arm around my shoulders and shakes me free of my rigidity.

I drew up his chair and sat down, seized with longing to take off my clothes and crawl into his bed, pull the blankets up tight, snuggle down into the sheets wrinkled by him, bury my face in his pillow and inhale the last vestiges of his smell, and then to fall into a deep, dreamless sleep.

I took the snapshot from the shelf and slipped it into my back pocket.

"Found anything?" Katrien asked when I came downstairs.

"I'd better be going," I said.

She went ahead of me to open the front door, rose up on her toes and kissed me on the cheek.

*

When I turned into the yard I saw Roland's car parked under the beech tree. I went inside, took my shoes off in the passage and paused by the dining room door. I could hear my cousin boasting about some deal he'd struck and my father's amused laughter.

"How did it go?" my mother asked when I came in. The three of them were having supper.

"How did it go… well, they're sad, understandably."

She poured me a cup of coffee. "I hope you passed on our condolences."

"They weren't there. Just the daughter."

She pushed the bread basket in my direction. "Go on, take."

"I'm not very hungry."

"He was always a bit of a weirdo," Roland said. "Attention-seeker, he was. All of them, really. I mean, that house of theirs, who'd want to live in a place like that?"

"You think everything's weird," I said.

"Now you two…" my father said soothingly.

"It's time you decided which clothes you want to take," my mother said. "You can leave the rest. I'll pack them for you."

167

"I'll do it later."

I went upstairs.

Roland made himself useful shifting furniture. There were still a couple of wardrobes and cabinets upstairs waiting to be moved to the back of the house.

"Watch out for that skirting board," I heard my mother cry. "We don't want to damage the wall. Anton, why don't you give us a hand."

I didn't respond.

"It's all right," my father said, "leave him be."

I set about taking down my posters. They were faded and reminded me too much of school. Patches of wallpaper came away with them, laying bare the pattern of my boyhood bedroom, the pale-blue clouds, lemon-yellow canaries, those grinning aeroplanes with propellers on their noses.

After stuffing the posters in the wastepaper basket, I turned to the wardrobe, but couldn't bring myself to sort through my shirts and sweaters because of all those invisible stains they bore which would be impossible to remove, so I shut the door again.

The others were sitting outside on the bench by the wall. Bottles were uncapped.

"Do you want a drink?" my mother called.

"No, Ma. Just leave me alone."

The starlings returned, flocking thickly around the tree and settling on the branches with a loud rustling like heavy rainfall.

"I can't get enough of watching those birds," I heard my father say.

I stood up, undressed, searched out my own warmth in the sheets, turned on my side and listened to the birds until I fell asleep.

CHAPTER 3

I WAS A LITTLE BOY again sitting in my high chair at the head of the table, out in the garden under the beech tree. It was a rainy day, the sky was overcast. Afternoon or early evening, could be either. But the overweening greyness, which might turn into drizzle any minute, did not match the happy atmosphere reigning all around me.

I saw myself banging my empty milk beaker on the tray of my high chair, to the rhythm of Alice and Aunt Odette clapping their hands. I remember my surprise at the sensation of the old comfort and warmth coming over me again, like a warm coat, a thick blanket, and the pleasure of seeing the Aunts' white hair coiffed with tortoiseshell combs over their ears and the intriguing little brooches of salamanders set with rubies climbing up the glossy black fabric of their blouses.

My father was conversing amicably with Michel, who'd hung his walking stick over the back of his chair. At my feet I could feel the dog wagging its tail under the table. It was only after I had glanced round all the faces there, gladly recognising each one above the table laden with dirty dishes and glasses with greasy fingerprints, that I noticed Willem sitting at the far end. He was wearing a dark suit and clinked his glass loudly against Flora's. They were laughing.

Then his eye caught mine. He nodded, nodded again and raised his glass to me. I could tell he was saying something, even as he laughed. His lips moved as if to ask, "Get it?"

He shook his head when Flora made to refill his glass.

"Willem!" I cried, but Aunt Odette hushed me with her hand on my arm.

"Just carry on," she murmured. "Go on, eat."

I drew back my arm, stood up in my chair, called his name a second time. Again I saw his lips move, and I shouted for him to speak up. He glared back at me.

"Hurry up," said Aunt Odette. "The food's getting cold."

She began to feed me soup by the spoonful, which seemed to take for ever, no matter how quickly I swallowed.

All around me people were rising from the table and putting away their folding chairs.

Raindrops fell on my bare arms. Someone grabbed me. I struggled to resist and felt as though I were falling.

*

I woke up on the edge of my bed. Outside, the horizon flashed with lightning. I got up, shut the window and went downstairs.

My mother was sitting at the kitchen table, in the light of a flickering lamp.

"Can't you sleep either?" she asked. "I'm getting to be just like my mother. She had trouble sleeping as she got older."

I passed behind her towards the cupboard, in search of a mug.

"Like some warm milk?"

"Yes, not too much, though."

There were some chocolate biscuits left in the tin, which I set down on the table.

"It's that friend of yours, isn't it?"

I nodded, chewed the inside of my cheek, dunked one of the biscuits into my milk.

"Ma?"

"Yes, lad?" She sniffed. In the lamplight her crows' feet seemed more deeply etched than ever.

"It's nothing really."

She sipped her milk. "Your Pa's snoring again. As soon as his head touches the pillow he's off."

I stared at her nose, which had a little dent halfway down it, just like mine, and at her lips, which she would press together and relax by turns when she was mulling things over, as if her thoughts were tweaking her facial muscles. My mother. The joints in her fingers were giving her trouble. Surgery hadn't helped. The growths kept coming back. I gazed at her blue-grey eyes, the remains of mascara on her lashes and thought: You don't know me. You're my mother, but you don't know me. You pressed me out of your body. I was a lump inside you, hanging on to your arteries, ruining your figure for the rest of your life, and you don't know me. You cleaned up my shit, powdered my bum. Ironed my shirts. Read the stains in my sheets like letters. Swaddled me, brushed my hair, cuddled me, mopped me up. And you don't know me.

"I'll be glad when we're out of this place for good," she said.

*

The thunderclouds had drifted away. I straightened the bed-clothes, but slept fitfully. Towards morning I started awake from a dream in which I was in a café in the market place in Ruizele, propping up the bar with a couple of classmates and Mr Bouillie. The atmosphere was joky, until the door opened and we saw Willem standing there in the harsh light, stark naked.

"What are you doing here?" I burst out in amazement.

He shot me one of his haughty looks, flicked little clouds of ash off his shoulders and said, "I'm back. Changed my mind."

*

Roland was having breakfast with my mother when I came downstairs.

"There's a letter for you," she said.

She had laid it beside my plate. I recognised the school crest. A blossoming branch entwined with the words *Saint Joseph*.

I ripped open the envelope and skimmed the letter from the corner of my eye: "tragic accident... snatched before his time... express our deepest sympathy for his parents... you are invited to attend the funeral service in class formation, as a fitting tribute to your fellow former pupil." It also suggested we bring one hundred francs to go towards a wreath.

I tore the letter into four pieces.

My mother was shocked. "You will be going, won't you?"

"I'll go on my own. I'll ask Pa for the car. He won't be needing it on Saturday, what with moving house."

"It's in the paper," Roland said. "It happened at the seaside. He'd been with relatives, I think."

"His aunt," I said.

"You should have seen that photograph, with the lorry, and that bike of his. Not a pretty picture."

172

"I want to go and see him... pay my respects," I said. "They brought him to the mortuary yesterday."

"Why don't you wait until your father gets back," my mother said. "He can drive you there."

"I don't want to wait until tonight. I'd rather go before it gets busy. It'll be quiet there now."

"You bet it will," Roland said, grinning.

I glared at him.

He cleared his throat, drank down his cup of coffee, and said in an apologetic tone, "You know what? I'll take you there if you like."

*

The antechamber of death. A low pavilion with a glass entrance flanked by rose beds and a sign saying MORTUARY planted among flowering lavender bushes.

A hall with a floor of gleaming granite and a counter behind which sits a young woman wearing demure make-up. At the request of each mourner she makes a brief call to some remote place in the depths of the building, where the dead are assembled on hard, straight-backed chairs, passing the time with back issues of magazines and desultory exchanges about the weather.

"I've come for De Vries," I said. "Willem de Vries."

Roland's shoes squealed on the floor behind me.

The young woman flicked the pages of a register, lifted the receiver and dialled an extension. She said we were to wait over there, in the waiting room across the corridor.

I heard her murmuring into the phone and noted a certain urgency in her tone, as if she were talking to him in person, telling him to comb his hair, to be sensible and mind his manners, and no, he was to put that comic away, he could return to it later.

The walls of the waiting room were decorated with photographs of hazy parkland landscapes. A little stack of solemn brochures lay on the table.

Thoughts at the graveside.

Callest Thou, Oh Lord?

On the cover a drawing of a hand and a heart crowned with thorns against a background of flames: See, I make everything whole again.

Roland stood with his back to me, staring out of the window at the car park.

People trooped down the corridor. Sniffling, coats being buttoned up. I heard the young woman intoning her professional condolences.

"It's them," Roland said. "I can see that sister of his. What's her name? Katrien…"

He swung round and moved away from the window.

The young woman came to fetch us. She accompanied us down the hall, until it branched off in a long corridor. "Sixth door on the right," she said, turning on her heel.

A soft drone of mournful music poured from speakers fitted in the ceiling. The doors were painted a dingy blue, with pearl-grey plastic handles that made me think of the reserved neutrality of doctors' surgeries; as if the dead might be holding office there for their relatives, with their hands loosely folded on the desk in front of them, smiling amicably and saying, "I was just watering my radishes. It started up here, in my chest. Can I offer you something to drink?"

Sixth door on the right. My courage sank to my shoes. My heart pounded in my throat.

Roland lagged behind. His eyes glinted anxiously in the dimly lit corridor. "If it's all the same to you I'd rather wait outside."

Looking the other way, he said, "Not my thing, to be honest. Freaks me out." He strode ahead to the end of the corridor, where a plant languished in a pot. "Sorry about that."

Him, scared. The killer of kittens. Squasher of butterflies.

I pushed open the door. From the ceiling emanated the same mournful music, seemingly to blot out the possibility that the dead might still be breathing, exhaling the last lingering air, like bubbles rising from a sinking bottle.

He lay in his coffin with purple cloths draped across his stomach and hands bandaged like stumps. They had dressed him in a cream-coloured shirt, which he wouldn't have been seen dead in when he was alive, not even for an exam—indeed, he used to go out of his way to buy the most garish Hawaii-print shirts he could find and equally ghastly ties, just to rile the teachers. There was something odd about the way the pale fabric was stretched taught across his chest, as if there were planks propping it up underneath.

His mouth was held shut with a bandage round his chin. His fair hair was for the most part tucked away, and in the glow of the spotlight illuminating his face, his cheeks showed signs of bruises and scratches under the generous coating of powder.

His skin was puffy, his lips swollen like the mouth of a river god in a Roman wall fountain. His forehead was creased, his eyebrows faintly wrinkled, as though he were sunk in thought about the extraordinary situation in which he found himself.

Next to a vase of arum lilies on a pedestal stood a glass of holy water and a palm frond. For a moment I pictured him blinking crossly at having water sprinkled on his face, sitting up, tearing off the bandage and raging, arms akimbo, "Hey you, what's going on?"—which was what he always did when I was offended and turned away to sulk and wallow in self-pity.

There was a timid knock on the door. From the corridor came the sound of Roland coughing and rattling his car keys.

I wiped my tears, leaned over and put my lips to Willem's forehead. The cold was unbearable.

I stepped out of the room, pulled the door behind me and left him to think things over.

CHAPTER 4

T HIS BODY, it could be the body of a stranger. It was only because it mimicked my every move so slavishly in shop windows and mirrors and revealed more and more of my father's face each time I shaved that I was moved to think: don't I know you? I'm sure I've seen you somewhere before.

This face staring back at me has the same closed, self-absorbed look as the house used to have on summer evenings when all the shutters were closed and, up at the top, under the roof, were the shadows of children having pillow fights and tripping across the floorboards long past bedtime.

Willem would be nearly forty now. Balding like his Pa, maybe, or sleek like his mother, settling contentedly into a looser-fitting body, spreading and warm like a well-worn sofa.

In death he is nineteen. Just left school. Passed his driving test. Proud of his first car. As if it would be any use to him now, in that place without echo or response.

My mother must have cut the photograph out of the paper, and I never got round to throwing it away. It turns up occasionally between the pages of books, sometimes fluttering down on to my lap. The reporter did not lack an eye for drama, for the picture shows the truck driver being led away by the police. There are several vans and an ambulance. A passer-by, hands clapped to her cheeks, surveys the white sheet on the kerb with a trouser leg plus trainer poking out from underneath, and the twisted wreck of his bike which is partially hidden by the wheels of the truck.

It can't have been more than half an hour after it happened. The body has yet to be released, the officers have yet to make their inquiries as to the cause of the accident. Someone has hastily covered him with the white of a shroud or christening robe.

For a long time I couldn't bring myself to imagine what he must have looked like lying under that sheet, even though I had seen him in his coffin afterwards. I clung to the idea that he had let himself fall backwards, the way he flopped on to the lawn at his parents' house on Fridays after school, with that enviable ability he had to exchange one world for another without a thought. It was like a miraculous postponement, like those few seconds of fierce concentration on the diving board during swimming class, before leaping into the air and falling into the chalice of water.

I still dream of him some nights. The images are becoming blurred, but the body is unmistakably his. His arms draw me close. His chest heaves calmly against my back. I feel the old rush of pleasure as his arms tighten their grip, gently but firmly, and then I wake up, only to find myself in the same bleak emptiness as on that Saturday when Roland drove into the yard in the early morning.

He had rented a van for transporting the heaviest items of furniture. I had lain awake most of the night, and watched the day dawn in its accustomed, lethargic way, peeling the darkness off the walls so that the place became awash with the vibrant red of an early autumn morning, quiet and compelling.

I got out of bed and went over to the window. I saw my cousin clamber down from the front of the van. He was wearing brown overalls with a zip up the front, and he whistled as he went round to unlock the back. My mother was already up; I'd heard her dry little cough as she passed my door on her way downstairs. Soon afterwards the smell of coffee floated from the kitchen through the rooms, most of which were already bare.

They noticed my sadness. Roland rambled on about which items would have to be loaded first and whether there were sufficient blankets and ropes to hand, while I sat and stared vacantly at the table in front of me, astounded that things could go on as if nothing had happened, that the world didn't stop and hold its breath, not even for a second. I could barely swallow a mouthful.

There was a silence when I left to go back upstairs, and I knew my father would be laying his hand on my mother's, that he would look at her and no doubt heave a deep sigh once I turned my back.

I sat on the edge of my bed. I could hear my mother going from room to room opening boxes, rummaging in them and shutting them again.

She pushed the door open and said, "I'll press a suit for you to wear, shall I?"

I could tell she was upset, and nodded.

"I'll do your grey one. It suits you so well. And you'd do better to wear your black shoes—I've given them a polish. They'll look better than the brown pair."

On my way to the bathroom, I passed Roland and my father in the passage, heaving a dresser between them. Roland was in front, and my father, red-faced, begged him to slow down by the step.

179

She'd put out an extra towel, and there was a bottle of eau de Cologne on the shelf beneath the mirror.

I turned on the taps and listened intently to the water rushing in the pipes, gurgling past the occasional bubble of trapped air. Then I poured soap into the tub and stirred the water to make foam.

My body hesitated as I stepped gingerly into the bath, avoiding contact with the tiles on the wall, and gave a little shudder as the warmth chased goose pimples up my arms.

I stretched out. Let myself slide under water, heard my skin rub against the sides.

"The first load's ready to go," Roland called out from downstairs. The doors of the van slammed, the engine revved, then the sound died away over the dyke.

They must have closed the coffin by now, I thought. Probably yesterday evening, last night maybe, who knows, perhaps it was happening at this very moment, with everyone there, his father, his mother, Katrien, all of them watching the shadow sliding across his forehead as the lid was lowered, without him raising his bandaged hands to fend it off.

I tried to lie completely still, like him, with the water covering me like a shield. I listened to the beating of my heart, until suddenly my body lunged upright with a great splash and my lungs filled themselves to bursting with an abandon that left me distraught.

I stood up and slipped my bathrobe on. Crossed over to the washbasin. Wet my cheeks. Rubbed shaving soap on them. Took the razor in my hands.

In the mirror I saw a haggard face with a snow-white beard. A body that seemed versed in being old and bent, shuffling down a corridor in a home somewhere in soggy slippers, dressing gown untied, complaining bitterly to the nurses for being late with breakfast. In his eyes a look of resignation which, over the years, had dulled every glint of former happiness and made it futile.

Willem loomed in my mind's eye. I became very angry. You've robbed me, I thought. You've stuffed my days in your inside pocket as if they were old letters, and next you'll hurl yourself on the fire like an old handbag.

*

I was almost done when there was a knock at the door and my father called my name.

"Come on in," I said, "I'm nearly ready anyway."

He had slung his vest over his shoulder, and was sweating profusely.

"That cousin of yours seems to think I'm a lad of twenty," he chuckled, and went on, "Take your time. I can wait."

I sat down on the lavatory seat, stared at nothing, rocked to and fro. I felt my testicles shrink, my stomach contract.

In spite of everything I felt sort of hungry. I'd have a slice of bread, I thought. Have a crap before leaving. Have another wash tonight. Cut my nails for the umpteenth time. Wipe my armpits with a towel. Brush my teeth. Routinely reflect that my ears were far too big. Time and again. Twice daily the small irritations of the oldest marriage in my personal history.

"Anton?"

My father was towelling himself dry.

I raised my eyes.

Our eyes met in the mirror.

"It'll pass, you know," he said.

My eyes prickled.

He bundled his towel on the rack self-consciously. Came towards me, took my chin in his hands.

After a pause he said, "Nothing you can do about it."

"I know."

He tried to strike a lighter note. "The least you can do for that poor boy is get a decent shave."

His thumb slid across my jaw, my lower lip.

"There's still some stubble."

He wet his hands, took the tube of shaving cream from the shelf and spread a fresh layer on my face.

"Chin up."

He steered my face to the right with his fingertips, then laid the razor against my cheek.

"You should just go with the flow. Follow the natural line, then you won't cut yourself so easily."

He touched the skin beneath my ear lobe and showed me his fingertip smeared with blood. He fumbled in his pockets for a cigarette paper to staunch the flow.

"I'll put some aftershave on it later," I said.

He knocked the foam off the razor, held it under the tap, resumed shaving. I could see his eyes narrowly following his fingers.

One day I would tell him things that would pain him as superficially as cuts from a razor blade, although the wounds would sting for longer. He would be left with questions that would itch like old mosquito bites every time he saw me arriving alone in my car, no kids to be scooped up from the back seat and hung around his shoulders like a garland of flowers. From that day on, too, he would suffer from niggling insecurities in his chest about having said too little to me or too much, while his silences spoke more volumes than entire libraries, enough for me to read for the rest of my life.

I watched him put the razor away and hold his hands under the tap. His stomach sagged over his trouser belt. The hair on his chest seemed to be thinning. He was a smooth, marbled pebble, all the sharpness worn down, gleaming in the sunlight. A safe place for him would be in the palm of my hand. I'd take good care of him.

He shook the drops off his fingers.

"At least you look respectable now," he said. "You'd better rinse that foam off your ears."

I stepped past him to the washbasin. Leaned over. He laid his hand on my back.

When I looked up he had gone.

*

The grey suit lay at the foot of my bed. It evoked a sense of expectation, the buzz of weddings or garden parties, which I found disturbing as I slipped my arms into the sleeves of the jacket with the shoulder pads that made me look twice as broad.

I put my shoes on. Double the lace to make a loop, tie the other end around it and pull it through to make a bow-knot. I could see myself in the changing room at school with Willem at my side, making fun of my embarrassment, showing me how.

I passed my mother in the corridor.

"I've taken your Pa's blue tie."

She turned up my shirt collar and laid the tie around my neck.

I felt myself turning into my father. As slim as he was on that day in October almost thirty years ago, when he strolled arm in arm with my mother in the gardens of the castle and stared at her veil melding with the mist rising from the grass by the lake. She was never younger than in that photograph.

I shivered, worried sick that my knees would buckle, later on, when the coffin slid away between the curtains into the furnace.

"Ma, why don't you come with me?" I asked, and regretted it instantly.

I saw her chewing her lower lip as she straightened my collar and tucked the end of the tie into my waistcoat.

"I don't think we'd want to go there, Anton. Anyway, we don't really know them very well, do we?"

I noted her shame. His father was an architect. Whenever my father found himself in the company of "posh folk", he would fold himself up like a newspaper left lying on a sofa.

"Forget it," I said.

She stood behind me, buffing the back of my jacket with a clothes brush.

"Spic and span."

I went downstairs.

"Here you are," my father said, handing me the car keys.

I stepped outside. Got behind the wheel. Switched on the ignition, reversed under the beech tree and rolled out of the yard.

By the gate stood my mother, signalling me to stop.

I wound the window down.

She leaned over and tucked a condolence card in my breast pocket.

"Don't forget to give this."

She patted the hair on my forehead.

"When will you be back? I'll keep some supper for you."

"That's fine, Ma."

"It'll be the other place." She was referring to the new house. "Mind you don't forget to go there, you don't want to be coming here by mistake. I know what you're like."

"All right."

I wound up the window. Waved. Drove out through the gate and up the road on the dyke. Sped away.

In the rear-view mirror I saw them both standing in the verge. My father had his arm around her waist.

He raised his hand. Shouted something.

I saw the pair of them receding gradually in the oblong mirror, the crown of the beech tree dwarfing the stables, and then, in a final glance before turning on to the motorway, it was all gone.

PUSHKIN PRESS

Pushkin Press was founded in 1997, and publishes novels, essays, memoirs, children's books—everything from timeless classics to the urgent and contemporary.

Our books represent exciting, high-quality writing from around the world: we publish some of the twentieth century's most widely acclaimed, brilliant authors such as Stefan Zweig, Marcel Aymé, Antal Szerb, Paul Morand and Yasushi Inoue, as well as compelling and award-winning contemporary writers, including Andrés Neuman, Edith Pearlman and Ryu Murakami.

Pushkin Press publishes the world's best stories, to be read and read again. Here are just some of the titles from our long and varied list:

═══

THE SPECTRE OF ALEXANDER WOLF
GAITO GAZDANOV

'A mesmerising work of literature' Antony Beevor

BINOCULAR VISION
EDITH PEARLMAN

'A genius of the short story' Mark Lawson, *Guardian*

TRAVELLER OF THE CENTURY
ANDRÉS NEUMAN

'A beautiful, accomplished novel: as ambitious as it is generous, as moving as it is smart' Juan Gabriel Vásquez, *Guardian*

BEWARE OF PITY
STEFAN ZWEIG

'Zweig's fictional masterpiece' *Guardian*

THE WORLD OF YESTERDAY
STEFAN ZWEIG

'*The World of Yesterday* is one of the greatest memoirs of the twentieth century, as perfect in its evocation of the world Zweig loved, as it is in its portrayal of how that world was destroyed' David Hare

JOURNEY BY MOONLIGHT
ANTAL SZERB

'Just divine… makes you imagine the author has had private access to your own soul' Nicholas Lezard, *Guardian*

BONITA AVENUE
PETER BUWALDA

'One wild ride: a swirling helix of a family saga… a new writer as toe-curling as early Roth, as roomy as Franzen and as caustic as Houellebecq' *Sunday Telegraph*

THE PARROTS
FILIPPO BOLOGNA

'A five-star satire on literary vanity… a wonderful, surprising novel' *Metro*

I WAS JACK MORTIMER
ALEXANDER LERNET-HOLENIA

'Terrific… a truly clever, rather wonderful book that both plays with and defies genre' Eileen Battersby, *Irish Times*

SONG FOR AN APPROACHING STORM
PETER FRÖBERG IDLING

'Beautifully evocative… a must-read novel' *Daily Mail*

THE RABBIT BACK LITERATURE SOCIETY
PASI ILMARI JÄÄSKELÄINEN

'Wonderfully knotty… a very grown-up fantasy masquerading as quirky fable. Unexpected, thrilling and absurd' *Sunday Telegraph*

RED LOVE: THE STORY OF AN EAST GERMAN FAMILY
MAXIM LEO

'Beautiful and supremely touching… an unbearably poignant description of a world that no longer exists' *Sunday Telegraph*

THE BREAK

PIETRO GROSSI

'Small and perfectly formed... reaching its end leaves the reader desirous to start all over again' *Independent*

FROM THE FATHERLAND, WITH LOVE

RYU MURAKAMI

'If Haruki is *The Beatles* of Japanese literature, Ryu is its *Rolling Stones*' David Pilling

BUTTERFLIES IN NOVEMBER

AUÐUR AVA ÓLAFSDÓTTIR

'A funny, moving and occasionally bizarre exploration of life's upheavals and reversals' *Financial Times*

BARCELONA SHADOWS

MARC PASTOR

'As gruesome as it is gripping... the writing is extraordinarily vivid... Highly recommended' *Independent*

THE LAST DAYS

LAURENT SEKSIK

'Mesmerising... Seksik's portrait of Zweig's final months is dignified and tender' *Financial Times*

BY BLOOD

ELLEN ULLMAN

'Delicious and intriguing' *Daily Telegraph*

WHILE THE GODS WERE SLEEPING

ERWIN MORTIER

'A monumental, phenomenal book' *De Morgen*

THE BRETHREN

ROBERT MERLE

'A master of the historical novel' *Guardian*